THE LAST WOMAN HE'D EVER DATE

BY

LIZ FIELDING

MILLS & BOON®

First published in Great Britain 2012
by Mills & Boon, an imprint of Harlequin (UK) Limited.
Large Print edition 2012
Harlequin (UK) Limited, Eton House,
18-24 Paradise Road, Richmond, Surrey TW9 1SR

© Liz Fielding 2012

ISBN: 978 0 263 22613 3

Printed and bound in Great Britain
by CPI Antony Rowe, Chippenham, Wiltshire

LP

With love

For my lovely daughter-in-law,
Veronique Allsopp-Hanskamp

CHAPTER ONE

Cranbrook Park for Sale?

THE future of the Cranbrook Park has been the subject of intense speculation this week after a move by HMRC to recover unpaid taxes sparked concern amongst the estate's creditors.

Cranbrook Park, the site of a 12th century Abbey, the ruins of which are still a feature of the estate, has been in continuous occupation by the same family since the 15th century. The original Tudor hall, built by Thomas Cranbrook, has been extended over the centuries and the Park, laid out in the late eighteenth century by Humphrey Repton, has long been at the heart of Maybridge society with both house and grounds generously loaned for charity events by the present baronet, Sir Robert Cranbrook.

The *Observer* contacted the estate office today for clarification of the situation, but no one was available for comment. —*Maybridge Observer,* Thursday 21 April

Sir Robert Cranbrook glared across the table. Even from his wheelchair and ravaged by a stroke he was an impressive man, but his hand shook as he snatched the pen his lawyer offered and signed away centuries of power and privilege.

'Do you want a sample of my DNA, too, boy?' he demanded as he tossed the pen on the table. His speech was slurred but the arrogant disdain of five hundred years was in his eyes. 'Are you prepared to drag your mother's name through the courts in order to satisfy your pretensions? Because I will fight your right to inherit my title.'

Even now, when he'd lost everything, he still thought his name, the baronetcy that went with it, meant something.

Hal North's hand was rock steady as he picked up the pen and added his signature to the papers, immune to that insulting 'boy.'

Cranbrook Park meant nothing to him except as a means to an end. He was the one in control here, forcing his enemy to sit across the table and look him in the eye, to acknowledge the shift in power. That was satisfaction enough.

Nearly enough.

Cranbrook's pawn, Thackeray, hadn't lived to witness this moment, but his daughter was now his tenant. Evicting her would close the circle.

'You can't afford to fight me, Cranbrook,' he said, capping the pen and returning it to the lawyer. 'You owe your soul to the tax man and without me to bail you out you'd be a common bankrupt man living at the mercy of the state.'

'Mr North…'

'I have no interest in claiming you as my father. You refused to acknowledge me as your son when it would have meant something,' he continued, ignoring the protest from Cranbrook's solicitor, the shocked intake of breath from around the room. It was just the two of them confronting the past. No one else mattered. 'I will not acknowledge you now. I don't need your name and I don't want your title. Unlike you, I did not have to wait for my father to die before I took my place in the world, to be a man.'

He picked up the deeds to Cranbrook Park. Vellum, tied with red ribbon, bearing a King's seal. Now his property.

'I owe no man for my success. Everything I am, everything I own, Cranbrook, including the estate you have squandered, lost because you were too idle, too fond of easy living to hold it, I have earned through hard work, sweat—things you've always thought beneath you. Things that could have served you. Would have saved you from this if you were a better man.'

'You're a poacher, a common thief…'

'And now I'm dining with presidents and prime ministers, while you're waiting for God in a world reduced to a single room with a view of a flower-bed instead of the park created by Humphrey Repton for one of your more energetic ancestors.'

Hal turned to his lawyer, tossed him the centuries-old deeds as casually as he would toss a newspaper in a bin and stood up, wanting to be done with this. To breathe fresh air.

'Think about me sitting at your desk as I make that world my own, Cranbrook. Think about my mother sleeping in the Queen's bed, sitting at the table where your ancestors toadied to kings instead of serving at it.' He nodded to the witnesses. 'We're done here.'

'Done! We're far from done!' Sir Robert Cranbrook clutched at the table, hauled himself to his feet. 'Your mother was a cheating whore who took the money I gave her to flush you away and then used you as a threat to keep her useless drunk of a husband in a job,' he said, waving away the rush to support him.

Hal North had not become a multimillionaire by betraying his emotions and he kept his face expressionless, his hands relaxed, masking the feelings boiling inside him.

'You can't blackmail an innocent man, Cranbrook.'

'She didn't have to be pushed very hard to come back for more. Years and years more. She was mine, bought and paid for.'

'Hal...' The quiet warning came from his lawyer. 'Let's go.'

'Sleeping in a bed made for a queen won't change what she is and no amount of money will make you anything but trash.' Cranbrook raised a finger, no longer shaky, and pointed at him. 'Your hatred of me has driven you all these years, Henry North and now everything you ever dreamed of has finally fallen into your lap and you think you've won.'

Oh, yes...

'Enjoy your moment, because tomorrow you're going to be wondering what there's left to get out of bed for. Your wife left you. You have no children. We are the same you and I...'

'Never!'

'The same,' he repeated. 'You can't fight your genes.' His lips curled up in a parody of a smile. 'That's what I'll be thinking about when they're feeding me through a tube,' he said as he collapsed back into the chair, 'and I'll be the one who dies laughing.'

Claire Thackeray swung her bike off the road and onto the footpath that crossed Cranbrook Park estate.

The No Cycling sign had been knocked down by the quad bikers before Christmas and late for work, again, she didn't bother to dismount.

She wasn't a rule breaker by inclination but no one was taking their job for granted at the moment. Besides, hardly anyone used the path. The Hall was unoccupied but for a caretaker and any fisherman taking advantage of the hiatus in occupancy to tempt Sir Robert's trout from the Cran wouldn't give two hoots. Which left only Archie and he'd look the other way for a bribe.

As she approached a bend in the path, Archie, who objected to anyone travelling faster than walking pace past his meadow, charged the hedge. It was terrifying if you weren't expecting it—hence the avoidance by joggers—and pretty unnerving if you were. The trick was to have a treat ready and she reached in her basket for the apple she carried to keep him sweet.

Her hand met fresh air and as she looked down she had a mental image of the apple sitting on the kitchen table, before Archie—not a donkey to be denied an anticipated treat—brayed his disapproval.

Her first mistake was not to stop and dismount the minute she realised she had no means of distracting him, but while his first charge had been a challenge, his second was the real deal. While she was still on the what, where, how, he leapt through one of the many gaps in the long-neglected hedge, easily clearing the sagging wire while she was too busy pumping the pedals in an attempt to outrun him to be thinking clearly.

Her second mistake was to glance back, see how far away he was and the next thing she knew she'd come to an abrupt and painful halt in a tangle of bike and limbs—not all of them her own—and was face down in a patch of bluebells growing beneath the hedge.

Archie stopped, snorted, then, job done, he turned around and trotted back to his hiding place to await his next victim. Unfortunately the man she'd crashed into, and who was now the bottom half of a bicycle sandwich, was going nowhere.

'What the hell do you think you're doing?' he demanded.

'Smelling the bluebells,' she muttered, keeping very still while she mentally checked out the 'ouch' messages filtering through to her brain.

There were quite a lot of them and it took her a while, but even so she would almost certainly have moved her hand, which appeared to be jammed in some part of the man's anatomy if it hadn't been trapped beneath the bike's handlebars. Presumably he was doing the same since he hadn't moved, either. 'Such a gorgeous scent, don't you think?' she prompted, torn between wishing him to the devil and hoping that he hadn't lost consciousness.

His response was vigorous enough to suggest that while he might have had a humour bypass—and honestly if you didn't laugh, well, with the sort of morning she'd had, you'd have to cry—he was in one piece.

Ignoring her attempt to make light of the situation he added, 'This is a footpath.'

'So it is,' she muttered, telling herself that he wouldn't have been making petty complaints about her disregard for the by-laws if he'd been seriously hurt. It wasn't a comfort. 'I'm so sorry I ran into you.' And she was. Really, really sorry.

Sorry that her broad beans had been attacked by a blackfly. Sorry that she'd forgotten Archie's apple. Sorry that Mr Grumpy had been standing in her way.

Until thirty seconds ago she had merely been late. Now she'd have to go home and clean up. Worse, she'd have to ring in and tell the news editor she'd had an accident which meant he'd send someone else to keep her appointment with the chairman of the Planning Committee.

He was going to be furious. She'd lived on Cranbrook Park all her life and she'd been assigned to cover the story.

'It's bad enough that you were using it as a race track—'

Oh, great. There you are lying in a ditch, entangled with a bent bicycle, with a strange man's hand on your backside—he'd better be trapped, too—and his first thought was to lecture her on road safety.

'—but you weren't even looking where you were going.'

She spat out what she hoped was a bit of twig.

'You may not have noticed but I was being chased by a donkey,' she said.

'Oh, I noticed.'

Not sympathy, but satisfaction.

'And what about you?' she demanded. Although her field of vision was small, she could see that he was wearing dark green coveralls. And she was pretty sure that she'd seen a pair of Wellington boots pass in front of her eyes in the split second before she'd crashed into the bank. 'I'd risk a bet you don't have a licence for fishing here.'

'And you'd win,' he admitted, without the slightest suggestion of remorse. 'Are you hurt?'

Finally...

'Only, until you move I can't get up,' he explained.

Oh, right. Not concern, just impatience. What a charmer.

'I'm so sorry,' she said, with just the slightest touch of sarcasm, 'but you shouldn't move after an accident.' She'd written up a first-aid course she'd attended for the women's page and was very clear on that point. 'In case of serious injury,' she added, to press home the point that he should be sympathetic. Concerned.

'Is that a fact? So what do you suggest? We just lie here until a paramedic happens to pass by?'

Now who was being sarcastic?

'I've got a phone in my bag,' she said. It was slung across her body and lying against her back out of reach. Probably a good thing or she'd have been tempted to hit him with it. What the heck did he think he was doing leaping out in front of her like that? 'If you can reach it, you could dial nine-nine-nine.'

'Are you hurt?' She detected the merest trace of concern so presumably the message was getting through his thick skull. 'I'm not about to call out the emergency services to deal with a bruised ego.'

No. Wrong again.

'I might have a concussion,' she pointed out. 'You might have concussion.' She could hope…

'If you do, you have no one but yourself to blame. The cycle helmet is supposed to be on your head, not in your basket.'

He was right, of course, but the chairman of the Planning Committee was old school. Any woman journalist who wanted a story had better be well-groomed and properly dressed in a skirt and high heels. Having gone to the effort of putting up her hair for the old misogynist, she wasn't about to ruin her hard work by crushing it with her cycle helmet.

She'd intended to catch the bus this morning. But if it weren't for the blackfly she could have caught the bus…

'How many fingers am I holding up?' Mr Grumpy asked.

'Oh…' She blinked as a muddy hand appeared in front of her. The one that wasn't cradling her back-side in a much too familiar manner. Not that she was about to draw attention to the fact that she'd noticed. Much wiser to ignore it and concentrate on the other hand which, beneath the mud, con-sisted of a broad palm, a well-shaped thumb, long fingers… 'Three?' she offered.

'Close enough.'

'I'm not sure that "close enough" is close enough,' she said, putting off the moment when she'd have to test the jangle of aches and move. 'Do you want to try that again?'

'Not unless you're telling me you can't count up to three.'

'Right now I'm not sure of my own name,' she lied.

'Does Claire Thackeray sound familiar?'

That was when she made the mistake of picking her face out of the bluebells and looking at him.

Forget concussion.

She was now in heart-attack territory. Dry mouth, loss of breath. Thud. Bang. Boom.

Mr Grumpy was not some irascible old bloke with a bee in his bonnet regarding the sanctity of footpaths—even if he was less than scrupulous about where he fished—and a legitimate griev-ance at the way she'd run him down.

He might be irritable, but he wasn't old. Far from it.

He was mature.

In the way that men who've passed the smooth-skinned prettiness of their twenties and fulfilled the potential of their genes are mature.

Not that Hal North had ever been pretty.

He'd been a raw-boned youth with a wild streak that had both attracted and frightened her. As a child she'd yearned to be noticed by him, but would have run a mile if he'd as much as glanced in her direction. As a young teen, she'd had fanta-sies about him that would have given her mother nightmares if she'd even suspected her precious girl of having such thoughts about the village bad boy.

Not that her mother had anything to worry about where Hal North was concerned.

She was too young for anything but the muddled fantasies in her head, much too young for Hal to notice her existence.

There had been plenty of girls of his own age, girls with curves, girls who were attracted to the aura of risk he generated, the edge of darkness that had made her shiver a little—shiver a lot—with feelings she didn't truly understand.

It had been like watching your favourite film star, or a rock god strutting his stuff on the television. You felt a kind of thrill, but you weren't sure what it meant, what you were supposed to do with it.

Or maybe that was just her.

She'd been a swot, not one of the 'cool' group in school who had giggled over things she didn't understand.

While they'd been practising being women, she'd been confined to experiencing it second-hand in the pages of nineteenth-century literature.

He'd bulked up since the day he'd been banished from the estate by Sir Robert Cranbrook after some particularly outrageous incident; what, she never discovered. Her mother had talked about it in hushed whispers to her father, but instantly switched to that bright, false change-the-subject smile if she came near enough to hear and she'd never had a secret-sharing relationship with any of the local girls.

Instead, she'd filled her diary with all kinds of fantasies about what might have happened, where he'd gone, about the day he'd return to find her all grown up—no longer the skinny ugly duckling but a fully fledged swan. Definitely fairy-tale material…

The years had passed, her diary had been abandoned in the face of increasing workloads from school and he'd been forgotten in the heat of a real-life romance.

Now confronted by him, as close as her girlish fantasy could ever have imagined, it came back in a rush and his power to attract, she discovered, had only grown over the years.

He was no longer a raw-boned skinny youth with shoulders he had yet to grow into, hands too big for his wrists. He still had hard cheekbones, though. A take-it-or-leave-it jaw, a nose that suggested he'd taken it once or twice himself. The only softness in his face, the sensuous curve of his lower lip.

It was his eyes, though, so dark in the shadow of

overhanging trees, which overrode any shortfall in classic good looks. They had the kind of raw energy that made her blood tingle, her skin goose, had her fighting for breath in a way that had nothing to do with being winded by her fall.

She reminded herself that she was twenty-six. A responsible adult holding down a job, supporting her child. A grown woman who did not blush. At all.

'I'm surprised you recognised me,' she said, doing her best to sound calm, in control, despite the thudding heart, racing pulse, the mud smearing her cheek. The fact that her hand was jammed between his legs. Nowhere near in control enough to admit the intimacy of a name she had once whispered over and over in the dark of her room.

She snatched her hand away, keeping her 'ouch' to herself as she scraped her knuckles on the brake lever and told herself not to be so wet.

'You haven't changed much.' His tone suggested that it wasn't a subject for congratulation. 'Still prim, all buttoned- up. And still riding your bike along this footpath. I'll bet it was the only rule you ever broke.'

'There's nothing big about breaking rules,' she said, stung into attack by his casual dismissal of her best suit. The suggestion that she still looked the same now as when she'd worn a blazer and a panama hat over hair braided in a neat plait. 'Nothing big about hiding under the willows, tickling Sir Robert's trout, either. Not the only rule you ever broke,' she added.

'Sharper tongued, though.'

That stung, too. The incident might have been painful but come on… She'd been chased by a donkey and every other man she knew would be at the very least struggling to hide a grin right now. Most would be laughing out loud.

'As for the trout,' he added, 'Robert Cranbrook never did own them, only the right to stand on the bank with a rod and fly and attempt to catch them. He can't even claim that now.'

'Maybe not,' she said, doing her best to ignore the sensory deluge, 'but someone can.' And sounded just as prim and buttoned-up as she apparently looked. 'HMRC if the rumours about the state of Sir Robert's finances are to be believed and the Revenue certainly won't take kindly to you helping yourself.'

Buttoned-up and priggish.

'Don't worry,' she said, making a determined effort to lighten the mood, 'I'll look the other way,

just this once, if you'll promise to ignore my mis-
demeanour.'

'Shall we get out of this ditch before you start
plea bargaining?' he suggested.

Plea bargaining? She'd been joking, for heaven's
sake! She wasn't that buttoned-up. She wasn't buttoned-up at all!

'You don't appear to have a concussion,' he continued, 'and unless you're telling me you can't feel
your legs, or you've broken something, I'd rather
leave the paramedics to cope with genuine emergencies.'

'Good call.' As an emergency it was genuine
enough—although not in the medical sense—but
if she was the subject of her own front-page story
she'd never hear the last of it in the newsroom.
'Hold on,' she said, not that he appeared to need
encouragement to do that. He hadn't changed that
much. 'I'll check.'

She did a quick round up of her limbs, flexing
her fingers and toes. Her shoulder had taken the
brunt of the fall and she knew that she would be
feeling it any moment now, but it was probably no
more than a bruise. The peddle had spun as her
foot had slipped, whacking her shin. She'd scraped
her knuckles on the brake lever and her left foot

appeared to be up to the ankle in the cold muddy water at the bottom of the ditch but everything appeared to be in reasonable working order.

'Well?' he demanded.

'Winded.' She wouldn't want him to think he was the cause of her breathing difficulties. 'And there will be bruises, but I have sufficient feeling below the waist to know where your hand is.'

He didn't seem to feel the need to apologise but then she had run into him at full tilt. She really didn't want to think about where he'd be black and blue. Or where her own hand had been.

'What about you?' she asked, somewhat belatedly.

'Can I feel my hand on your bum?'

The lines bracketing his mouth deepened a fraction and her heart rate which, after the initial shock of seeing him, had begun to settle back down, thudding along steadily with only an occasional rattle of the cymbals, took off on a dramatic drum roll.

CHAPTER TWO

'ARE you in one piece?' Claire asked, doing her best to ignore the timpani section having a field day and keep it serious.

If he could do that with an almost smile, she wasn't going to risk the full nine yards.

'I'll survive.'

She sketched what she hoped was a careless shrug. 'Close enough.'

And this time the smile, no more than a dare-you straightening of the lips, reached his eyes, setting her heart off on a flashy drum solo.

'Shall we risk it, then?' he prompted when she didn't move.

'Sorry.' She wasn't an impressionable teenager, she reminded herself. She was a grown woman, a mother… 'I'm still a bit dazed.' That, at least, was true. Although whether the fall had anything to do with it was a moot point. Forget laughing about this. Hal North was a lot safer when he was being a grouch.

'Okay,' he said. 'Let's try this. You roll to your right and I'll do my best to untangle us both.'

She gingerly eased herself onto her shoulder, then gave a little gasp at the unexpected intimacy of his cold fingers against the sensitive, nylon-clad flesh as he hooked his hand beneath her knee. It was a lifetime since she was that timid girl who'd watched him from a safe distance, nearly died when he'd looked at her, but he was still attracting and scaring her in equal quantities. Okay, maybe not quite equal…

'Does that hurt?' he asked.

'No!' She was too fierce, too adamant and his eyes narrowed. 'Your hand was cold,' she said lamely as he lifted her leg free of the frame.

'That's what happens when you tickle trout,' he said, confirming her impression that he'd just stepped up out of the stream when she ran into him. It would certainly explain why she hadn't seen him. And why he hadn't had time taking avoiding action.

'Are you still selling your catch to the landlord of The Feathers?' she asked, doing her best to control the conversation.

'Is he still in the market for poached game?' he asked, not denying that he'd once supplied him through the back door. 'He'd have to pay rather more for a freshly caught river trout these days.'

'That's inflation for you. I hope your rod is still in one piece.'

His eyebrow twitched, proving that he did, after all, possess a sense of humour. 'Couldn't you tell?'

'Your fishing rod…' Claire stopped, but it was too late to wish she'd ignored the innuendo.

'It's not mine,' he said, taking pity on her. 'I confiscated it from a lad fishing without a licence.'

'Confiscated it?'

As he sat up, she caught sight of the Cranbrook crest on the pocket of his coveralls. He was working on the estate? Poacher turned gamekeeper? Why did that feel so wrong? He would be a good choice if the liquidators wanted to protect what assets remained. He knew every inch of the estate, every trick in the book…

'Aren't they terribly expensive?' she asked. 'Fishing rods.'

'He'll get it back when he pays his fine.'

'A fine? That's a bit harsh,' she said, rather afraid she knew who might have been trying his luck. 'He's only doing what you did when you were his age.'

'The difference being that I was bright enough not to get caught.'

'I'm not sure that's something to be proud of.'

'It beats the hell out of the alternative.' She couldn't argue with that. 'I take it, from all this touching concern, that you know the boy?'

'I imagine it was Gary Harker. His mother works in the estate office. She's at her wit's end. He left school last year and hasn't had a sniff of a job. In the old days he'd have been taken on by the estate,' she prompted. 'Learned a skill.'

'Working for the gentry for a pittance.'

'Minimum wage these days. Not much, but a lot better than nothing. If the estate is hiring, maybe you could put a good word in for him?'

'You don't just want me to let him off, you want me to give him a job, too?' he asked.

'Maybe there's some government-sponsored apprenticeship scheme?' she suggested. 'I could find out. Please, Hal, if I talk to him, will you give him a break?'

'If I talk to him, will you give me one?' he replied.

'I'll do better than that.' She beamed, aches and pains momentarily forgotten. 'I'll bake you a cake. Lemon drizzle? Ginger? Farmhouse?' she tempted and for a moment she seemed to hold his attention. For a moment she thought she had him.

'Don't bother,' he said, breaking eye contact, turning back to her bike. 'The front wheel's bent out of shape.'

She swallowed down her disappointment. 'Terrific. For want of an apple the bike was lost,' she said, as he propped it against a tree. 'Can it be straightened out?'

'Is it worth it?' he asked, reaching out a hand to help her up. 'It must be fifty years old.'

'Older,' she replied, clasping his hand. 'It belonged to Sir Robert's nanny.'

His palm was cold, or maybe it was her own that was hot. Whatever it was, something happened to her breathing as their thumbs locked around each other and Hal braced himself to pull her up onto the path. A catch, a quickening, as if his power was flooding into her, his eyes heating her from the inside out.

Just how reliable was the finger test as a diagnosis of concussion, anyway?

'I've got you,' he said, apparently feeling nothing but impatience, but as he pulled, something caught at the soft wool of her jacket, holding her fast.

'Wait!' She'd already wrecked her bike and she

wasn't about to confound the situation by tearing lumps out of her one good suit. 'I'm caught on something.' She yelped as she reached back to free herself and her hand snagged on an old, dead bramble, thorns hard as nails. 'Could my day get any worse?' she asked, sucking at the line of tiny scarlet spots of blood oozing across the soft pad at the base of her thumb.

'That depends on whether your tetanus shots are up to date.'

Was that, finally, a note of genuine concern? Or was it merely the hope she would need a jab— something to put the cherry on top of her day— that she heard in his voice?

'That was a rhetorical question,' she replied, tired of being on the defensive, 'but thanks for your concern.' And he could take that any way he chose.

Right now she'd gladly suffer a jab that would offer a vaccination against dangerous men. The kind that stood in your way on footpaths, made you say blush-making things when you hadn't blushed in years. Made you feel thirteen again.

Made you feel…

'Here. Use this,' he said as she searched her pockets for a tissue. He dropped a freshly ironed handkerchief into her lap then, as he stepped down into the ditch to unhook her from the thorns, he spoiled this unexpected gallantry by saying, 'You really should make an attempt to get up earlier.'

She turned to look at him. 'Excuse me?'

He was closer than she realised and his chin, rough with an overnight growth of beard, brushed against her cheek. It intensified the tingle, sent her temperature up a degree. Deadly dangerous. She should move.

Closer…

'It's gone nine,' he pointed out. 'I assumed you were late for work?'

His hair was dark and thick. He'd worn it longer as a youth, curling over his neck, falling sexily into his eyes. These days it was cut with precision. Even the tumble into the ditch had done no more than feather a cowlick across his forehead. And if possible, the effect was even more devastating.

'I am,' she admitted, 'but not because I overslept.'

His breath was warm against her temple and her skin seemed to tingle, as if drawn by his closeness.

She really should move. Put some distance between them.

She'd never been close enough to see the colour of his eyes before. They were very dark and she'd always imagined, in her head, they were the blue-grey of wet slate, but in this light they seemed to be green. Or was it simply the spring bright tunnel of leaves that lent them a greenish glow?

He raised an eyebrow as he opened a clasp knife. 'You had something more interesting to keep you in bed?'

'You could say that.' In her vegetable bed, any-way, but if he chose to think there was a man in-terested in undoing her buttons she could live with that. 'I'm more concerned about my ten o'clock appointment at the Town Hall with the chairman of the Planning Committee.'

He glanced at his watch. 'You're not going to make it.'

'No.' There were worst things than crashing into a ditch and losing her job was one of them. 'If you got a move on I could call him before I'm late and reschedule for later today.'

'Have a care, Miss Thackeray,' he warned, glanc-ing up at her, 'or I'll leave you where you are.'

About to point out that all she had to do was undo her jacket and she could free herself, she thought better of it.

If Hal North was working for the estate he probably knew far more than the planning department about what was going on.

'I was going to talk to him about the Cranbrook Park estate,' she said, moving her hand away from her jacket button. 'There's a rumour going round that a property developer has bought it.'

The rumour of a sale was real enough. As for the rest, she was just fishing and most people couldn't wait to tell you that you were wrong, tell you what they knew.

'And why would that be of interest to you?'

Yes, well, Hal North hadn't been like most boys and it seemed he wasn't like most men, either.

'The estate is my landlord,' she said. 'I have a vested interest in what happens to it.'

'You have a lease.'

'Well, yes…' With barely three months left to run. 'But I've known Sir Robert since I was four years old. I can't expect a new owner to have the same concern for his tenants. He might not want to renew it and if he did, he'll certainly raise the rent.' Something else to worry about. It was vital she keep her job. 'And then there are the rumours about a light industrial estate at my end of the village.'

'Not in my backyard?' he mocked.

'Yours, too,' she replied, going for broke. 'I live in Primrose Cottage.'

'What about the jobs that light industry would bring to the area?' he replied, apparently unmoved by the threat to his childhood home. 'Don't you care about that angle? What about young Gary Harker?'

'I'm a journalist.' A rather grand title for someone working on the news desk of the local paper. 'I'm interested in all the angles. Protecting the countryside has its place, too.'

'For the privileged few.'

'The estate has always been a local amenity.'

'Not if you're a fisherman,' he reminded her. 'I assume, since you're covering local issues that you work for the local rag?'

'The *Observer*, yes,' she said, doing her best to ignore his sarcasm, keep a smile on her face. She wanted to know what he knew.

'All that expensive education and that's the best you could do?'

'That's an outrageous thing to say!'

Oops… There went her smile.

But it explained why, despite the fact that she'd been a skinny kid, totally beneath his notice, he had remembered her. Her pink and grey Dower

House school uniform had stood out amongst the bright red Maybridge High sweatshirts like a lily on a dung heap. Or a sore thumb. Depending on your point of view.

The other children in the village had mocked her difference. She'd pretended not to care, but she'd envied them their sameness. Had wanted to be one of them, to belong to that close-knit group clustered around the bus stop every morning when she was driven past in the opposite direction.

'You were headed for Oxbridge according to your mother. Some high-flying media job.'

'Was I?' she asked, as if she didn't recall every moment of toe-curling embarrassment as her mother held forth in the village shop. She might have been oblivious, but Claire had known that they were both the object of derision. 'Obviously I wasn't as bright as she thought I was.'

'And the real reason?'

She should be flattered that he didn't believe her, but it only brought back the turmoil, the misery of a very bad time.

'It must have been having a baby that did it.' If he was back in the village he'd find out soon enough. 'Miss Snooty Smartyhat brought down to size by her hormones. It was a big story at the time.'

'I can imagine. Anyone I know? The father?' he added, as if she didn't know what he meant.

'There aren't many people left in the village who you'll remember,' she said, not wanting to go there. Even after all these years the crash of love's young dream as it hurtled to earth still hurt… 'As you pointed out, there aren't any jobs on the estate for our generation.' Few jobs for anyone. Sir Robert's fortunes had been teetering on the brink for years. Cheap imports had ruined his business and with his factories closed, the estate—a money sink— had lost the income which kept it going.

The Hall was in desperate need of repair. Some of the outbuildings were on the point of falling down and many of the hedges and fences were no longer stock proof.

Cue Archie.

'No one who'll remember me is what I think you mean,' he said.

'You're in luck, then.'

'You think I'd be unwelcome?'

He appeared amused at the idea and flustered, she said, 'No…I just meant…'

'I know what you meant,' he said, turning back to the delicate task of unpicking the threads of her suit from the thorns.

Ignoring the cold and damp that was seeping through her skirt, trying to forget just how much she disliked this part of her job, she tried again. This time, however, since he clearly wasn't going to be coaxed into indiscretion, she came right out and asked him.

'Can you tell me what's happening to the estate?' Maybe the subtle implication that he did not know himself would provoke an answer.

'There'll be an announcement about its future in the next day or two. I imagine your office will get a copy.'

'It has been sold!' That wasn't just news, it was a headline! Brownie points, job security… 'Who's the new owner?'

'Do you want a scoop for the *Observer,* Claire?' The corner of his mouth quirked up in what might have been a smile. Her stomach immediately followed suit. She might be older and wiser, but he'd always had a magnetic pull. 'Or merely gossip for the school gates?'

'I'm a full-time working single mother,' she said, doing her best to control the frantic jangle of hormones that hadn't been disturbed in years. 'I don't have time to gossip at the school gates.'

'Your baby's father didn't stick around, then?'

'Well spotted. Come on, Hal,' she pleaded. 'It's obvious that you know something.'

If he had been the chairman of the Planning Committee she'd have batted her eyelashes at him. As it was, she'd barely raised a flutter before she regretted it.

Hal North was not a man to flirt with unless you meant it.

Poised on the brink of adolescence, paralysed with shyness if he so much as glanced in her direction, she had not fully understood the danger a youth like Hal North represented.

As a woman, she didn't have that excuse.

'It'll be public knowledge soon enough,' she pressed, desperately hoping that he wouldn't have noticed.

'Then you won't have long to wait will you?'

'Okay, no name, but can you tell me what's going to happen to the house?' That's all she'd need to grab tomorrow's front page. 'Is it going to be a hotel and conference centre?'

'I thought you said it was going to be a building site. Or was it an industrial estate?'

'You know how it is…' She attempted a careless shrug, hiding her annoyance that he persisted in trading question for question. She was supposed to be the professional, but he was getting all the answers. 'In the absence of truth the vacuum will be filled with lies, rumour and drivel.'

'Is that right?' He straightened, put away his knife. 'Well, you'd know more about that than me.'

'Oh, please. I work for a local newspaper. We might publish rumour, and a fair amount of drivel, but we're too close to home to print lies.'

She made a move to get up, eager now to be on her way, but he forestalled her with a curt 'wait.'

Assuming that he could see another problem, she obeyed, only to have him put his hands around her waist.

She should have protested, would have protested if the connection between her brain and her mouth had been functioning. All that emerged as he picked her bodily out of the ditch was a huff of air, followed by a disgusting squelch as her foot came out of the mud, leaving her shoe behind. Then she found herself with her nose pressed against the dark green heavyweight cloth of his coveralls and promptly forgot all about the bluebells.

Hal North had a scent of his own. Mostly fresh air, the sweet green of crushed grass and new dandelion leaves, but something else was coming through that fresh laundry smell. The scent of a man who'd been working. Warm skin, clean sweat—unexpectedly arousing—prickling in her nose.

He was insolent, provoking and deeply, deeply disturbing but, even as the urgent 'no!' morphed into an eager 'yes…' she told herself to get a grip. He had been bad news as a youth and she'd seen, heard nothing to believe that had changed.

'If you'll excuse me,' she said, doing her best to avoid meeting those dangerous eyes as she clung to his shoulders, struggling for balance and to get her tongue and teeth to line up to form the words. 'I really have to be going.'

'Going? Haven't you forgotten something?'

'My shoe?' she suggested, hoping that he'd dig it out of the mud for her. He was, after all, dressed for the job. While the prospect of stepping back into it was not particularly appealing, she wasn't about to mess up the high heels she carried in the messenger bag slung across her back.

'I was referring to the fact that you cycled along a footpath, Claire. Breaking the by-laws without a second thought.'

'You're kidding.' She laughed but the arch lawbreaker of her youth didn't join in. He was not kidding. He was… She didn't know what he was.

She only knew that he was looking down at her with an intensity that was making her pulse race. 'No! No, you're right,' she said, quickly straightening her face. 'It was very wrong of me. I won't do it again.'

The hard cheekbones seemed somehow harder, the jaw even more take it or leave it, if that were possible.

'I don't believe you.'

'You don't?' she asked, oblivious to the demands of the front page as her upper lip burned in the heat of eyes that were not hard. Not hard at all. Her tongue flicked over it, in an unconscious attempt to cool it. 'What can I do to convince you?'

The words were out of Claire's mouth, the harm done, before she could call them back and one corner of his mouth lifted in a 'got you' smile.

There was no point in saying that she hadn't meant it the way it had sounded. He wouldn't believe that, either. She wasn't sure she believed it herself.

If it looked like an invitation, sounded like an invitation…

Her stomach clenched in a confused mix of fear and excitement as, for one heady, heart-stopping moment she thought he was going to take her up on it. Kiss her, sweep her up into his arms, fulfil every girlish dream she'd confided to her journal. Back in the days before she'd met Jared, when being swept into Hal's arms and kissed was the limit of her imagination.

No! What was she thinking!

In a move that took him by surprise, she threw up her arm, stepped smartly back, out of the circle of his hands, determined to put a safe distance between them before her wandering wits made a complete fool of her. But the day wasn't done with her.

The morning was warm and sunny but it had rained overnight and her foot, clad only in fine nylon—no doubt in shreds—didn't stop where she'd put it but kept sliding backwards on the wet path. Totally off balance, arms flailing, she would have fallen if he hadn't caught her round the waist in a grip that felt less like rescue than capture and her automatic thanks died in her throat.

'You've cycled along that path every day this week,' he said, in a tone that suggested he was right, 'and I don't think you're going to stop without good reason.'

'Archie is a great deterrent,' she managed.

'Not to those of us who know his weakness for

apples. A weakness I've seen you take advantage of more than once this week. Being late appears to be something of a habit with you.'

He'd seen her? When? How long had he been back? More importantly why hadn't she heard about it when she called in at the village shop? There might be few people left who would remember bad, dangerous, exciting Hal North, but the arrival of a good-looking man in the neighbourhood was always news.

'Were you lying in wait for me today?'

'I have better things to do with my time, believe me. I'm afraid this morning you just ran out of luck.'

'And here was me thinking I'd run into you.' He moved his head in a gesture that suggested it amounted to the same thing. 'So? What are you going to do?' she demanded, in an attempt to keep the upper hand. 'Call the cops?'

'No,' he said. 'I'm going to issue an on-the-spot penalty fine.'

She laughed, assuming that he was joking. He didn't join in. Not joking…

'Can you do that?' she demanded and when he didn't answer the penny finally dropped. A fine… 'Oh, right. I get it.'

He hadn't changed. His shoulders might be broader, he might be even more dangerously attractive than the boy who'd left the village all those years ago, but inside, where it mattered, he was still the youth who'd poached the Park game, torn up the park on his motorcycle, sprayed graffiti on Sir Robert's factory walls. Allegedly. No one had ever caught him.

He was back now as gamekeeper, warden, whatever and he apparently considered this one of the perks of the job.

She shrugged carelessly in an attempt to hide her disappointment as she dug around in her bag, fished out her wallet.

'Ten pounds,' she said, flicking it open. 'It's all I have apart from small change. Take it or leave it.'

'I'll leave it.' Her relief came a fraction too soon. 'I'm looking for something a little more substantial by way of payment.' What! 'Something sufficiently memorable to ensure that the next time you're tempted to ride along this path, you'll think again.'

She opened her mouth to protest that parting with all the spare cash she had to see her through until the end of the month was memorable enough, thank you very much. All that emerged was another of those wordless huffs as he pulled her against him, expelling the air from her body as her hips collided with hard thighs.

For a moment she hung there, balanced on her toes.

For a moment he looked down at her.

'What would make you think again, Claire?'

Had she thought there was anything soft about those eyes? She was still wondering how she could have got that so wrong when his mouth came down on hers with an abrupt, inescapable insistence.

It was outrageous, shocking, disgraceful. And everything she had ever imagined it would be.

CHAPTER THREE

CLAIRE Thackeray abandoned her bike, her shoe and, as her hair descended untidily about her shoulders, a scatter of hair pins.

Hal knew that he would have to go after her, but it hadn't taken her stunned expression, or her stiff back as she limped comically away from him on one shoe to warn him that laughing would be a mistake.

It was as clear as day that nothing he did or said would be welcome right now, although whether her anger was directed at him or herself was probably as much a mystery to her as it was to him.

The only thing he knew with certainty was that she would never again ride her bike along this path. Never toss an apple—the toll Archie charged for letting her pass unmolested on her bike—over the hedge.

'Job done, then,' he muttered as, furious with himself, furious with her, he stepped down into the ditch to recover the shoe she'd left embedded in the mud. He tossed it into the basket on the front of her bike, grabbed the fishing rod he'd confiscated from Gary Harker and followed her.

It was the first time he'd lost control in years and he'd done it not just once, but twice. First when he'd kissed her, and then again as her unexpected meltdown had made him forget that his intention had been to punish her. Punish her for her insulting offer of a bribe. Her pitiful attempt at seducing what he knew out of him. Most of all, to punish her for being a Thackeray.

He'd forgotten everything in the softness of her lips unexpectedly yielding beneath his, the silk of her tongue, the heat ripping through him as she'd clung to him in a way that belied all that buttoned-up restraint.

Which of them came to their senses first he could not have said. He only knew that when he took a step back she was looking at him as if she'd run into a brick wall instead of a flesh-and-blood man.

Any other woman who'd kissed him like that would have been looking at him with soft, smoky eyes, her cheeks flushed, her mouth smiling with anticipation, but Claire Thackeray had the look of a rabbit caught in headlights and, beneath the smear of mud, her cheek had been shockingly white.

Her mouth was swollen but there was no smile and she hadn't said a word. Hadn't given him a chance to say... What?

I'm sorry?

To the daughter of Peter Thackeray? The girl who'd been too good to mix with the village kids. The woman who, even now, down on her luck and living in the worst house on the estate, was still playing the patronising lady bountiful, just as her mother had. Handing out charity jobs to the deserving poor. Sending the undeserving to the devil...

That wasn't how it was meant to be.

But she hadn't waited for an apology.

After that first stricken look, she'd turned around and walked away from him without a word, without a backward glance as if he was still the village trash her father—taking his cue from Sir Robert—had thought him. As if she was still the Cranbrook estate's little princess.

The battered wheel ground against the mudguard and stuck, refusing to move another inch. Cursing the wretched thing, he propped it up out of sight behind a tree, then grabbing her shoe he strode after her.

'Claire! Wait, damn it!'

* * *

Claire wanted to die.

No, that was ridiculous. She wasn't an idiot kid with a crush on the local bad boy. She was a responsible, sensible grown woman. Who wanted to die.

How dare he!

Easy… Hal North had always done just what he wanted, looked authority in the eye and dared anything, defying them to do their worst.

How could she?

How could she just stand there and let Hal North kiss her? Respond as if she'd been waiting half her life for him to do exactly that? Even now her senses were alight with the heat of it, the blood thundering around her body at the thrill of surrendering to it, letting go in a world-well-lost moment when nothing else mattered. Not her dignity, not her child…

It had been everything her youthful imagination had dreamt about and more. Exhilarating, a dream-come-true moment to rival anything in a fairy tale.

Appalling.

She clung desperately to that word, closing her eyes in a vain attempt to blot out the warm, animal scent of his skin, the feel of his shoulders, solid beneath her hands as she'd clutched at them for support. The taste of his hard mouth lighting her up as if she'd been plugged into the national grid; softening from punishing to seductively tender as her lips had surrendered without a struggle to the silk of his tongue.

'Didn't you hear me?'

Of course she'd heard him.

"Wait, damn it…"

He'd sounded angry.

Why would he be angry? He was the one who'd kissed her without so much as a by-your-leave…

'I brought your shoe,' he said.

She took it from him without slowing down, without looking at him. It was caked in wet sticky mud and she tossed it defiantly back into the ditch.

'That was stupid.'

'Was it?' Probably. Undoubtedly. She'd come back and find it later. 'What's your on-the-spot fine for littering?'

'Are you sure you want to know?'

She stubbed her toe on a root and he caught her arm as she stumbled.

'Get lost, Hal,' she said, attempting to shake him off. He refused to be shaken and she glared up at him. 'Are you escorting me off the premises?'

Bad choice of words, she thought as his mouth tightened.

'It's for your own safety.'

'Safety? Archie isn't going to bother me now I'm on foot, but who's going to keep me safe from you?' she demanded, clearly not done with 'stupid.'

'You've had a shock,' he replied, all calm reason, which just made her all the madder.

'Now you're concerned!'

Too right she'd had a shock. She'd had a shock right down to her knees but it had nothing to do with Archie and everything to do with crashing into Hal North. Everything to do with the fact that he'd kissed her. That she'd kissed him back as if she'd been waiting to do that all her life. Maybe she had…

How dare he be all calm reason when she was a basket case?

'It's a bit late to start playing knight errant don't you think?'

'You're mistaking me for someone else.'

'Not in a hundred years,' she muttered, catching her breath as she stepped on a sharp stone, gritting her teeth to hold back the expletive, refusing to let him see that she was in pain.

The last thing she needed was a smug I-told-you-so from Hal North.

It did have the useful side effect of preventing her from saying anything else she'd regret when Hal moved his hand from her arm and looped it firmly around her waist, taking her weight so that she had no choice but to lean into the solid warmth of his body, allow him to support her.

The alternative was fighting him which would only make things worse as she limped the rest of the way home, her head against his shoulder, her cheek against the hard cloth of his overalls. The temptation was to simply surrender to the comfort, just as she'd surrendered to his kiss and it took every crumb of concentration to mentally distance herself from the illusion of safety, of protection and pray that he'd put her erratic breathing down to 'shock.'

When they reached her gate, she allowed herself to relax and took the fishing rod when he handed it to her, assuming he meant her to give it back to Gary.

'Thank you...' The word ended in a little shriek as he bent and caught her behind the knees, scooping her up like some bride being carried over the threshold. Hampered by the rod, she could do nothing but fling an arm around his neck and hang on as he strode along the gravel path that led around the house to the back door.

'Key?' he prompted, as he deposited her with an equal lack of ceremony on the doorstep.

'I'm home. Job done,' she said, propping the rod by the door, waiting for him to leave. She was damned if she was going to say thank you again.

'Are you going to be difficult?' he asked.

'You bet.'

He shrugged, glanced around, spotted the brick where she hid her spare key. 'My mother used to keep it in the same place,' he said, apparently oblivious to her huff of annoyance as he retrieved it and opened the door. 'In fact, I'm pretty sure it's the same brick.'

'Go away,' she said, kicking off her remaining shoe in the scullery where the boots and coats were hung.

'Not before the statutory cup of hot, sweet tea,' he said, following her inside and easing off his own boots.

Her suit was damp and muddy, her foot was throbbing and her body, a jangle of sore, aching bits demanding her attention now that she'd come to a halt, responded with a tiny 'yes, please' whimper. She ignored it.

'I don't take sugar.'

'I do.'

Behind her, the phone began to ring. She ignored it for as long as she could, daring him to take another step then, with what she hoped was a careless shrug—one that her shoulder punished her for—she limped, stickily, into the kitchen and lifted the receiver from the cradle.

'Claire Thack...'

Hal pulled out a chair, tipped off the two sleeping cats and, taking her arm, eased her down into it before crossing to the kettle.

'Claire?'

'Oh, Brian...'

'Is there a problem?' Brian Gough, the news editor, sounded concerned rather than annoyed, but then she had always striven to be one hundred per cent reliable—hoarding those Brownie points that every working mother needed against the days when her daughter was sick and her needs had to come before everything, even the desperate necessity of making a career for herself. 'Only I've just had Charlie on the phone.'

Charlie... That would be Charlie Peascod, the

Chief Planning Officer. Her important ten o'clock meeting. She caught sight of the clock and groaned.

Hal heard her and turned. 'Are you okay?' he asked, with what appeared to be genuine concern.

'No,' she hissed, swivelling round so that her back was to him in an effort to concentrate. 'I'm s-o s-sorry, Brian but I've had a bit of an accident.'

'An accident? What kind of accident? Are you all right?'

'Y-yes…' she said as, without warning, she began to shiver.

'You don't sound it.'

'I will be.' Behind her there was a world of comfort in the sound of the kettle being filled. The sound of the biscuit tin lid being opened. She refused to look… 'I was going to c-call you but…' But it had gone clean out of her head. Her important meeting, her job, pretty much everything. That's what a man like Hal North could do to you with nothing more than a kiss. 'I f-fell off my bike.'

'Have you been to the hospital?' he asked, seriously concerned now, which only added to her guilt.

'It's not that bad, truly.' And it wasn't. She just needed to get a grip, pull herself together. 'Just the odd bump and scrape, but there was rather a lot of mud,' she said, attempting to make light of it. 'Once I've had a quick shower I'll be out of here. With luck I'll catch the eleven o'clock bus.'

'No, no… These things can shake you up. We can manage without you.'

Her immediate reaction was to protest—that was so not something she wanted to hear—but for some reason she appeared to be shaking like a jelly. If she hadn't been sitting down, she would almost certainly have collapsed in heap.

'Take the rest of the week off, put your feet up. We'll see you on Monday.'

'If you insist,' she said, just to be sure that he was telling her, she wasn't begging. 'I'll call Mr Peascod now to apologise. Reschedule for Monday.'

'Oh, don't worry about Charlie. I'm taking him to lunch and, let's face it, he's much more likely to be indiscreet after a glass of wine.'

Of course he was. All boys together. On the golf course or down the pub. No need for Brian Gough to make an effort with his hair, wear his best suit, flutter his eyelashes. He'd take Charlie to the King's Head and over a plate of their best roast beef—on expenses—he'd hear all about what was going on at Cranbrook Park. It was how it had always been done.

Forget the news desk. At this rate, she'd be writing up meetings of the Townswomen's Guild, reviewing the Christmas panto until she was drawing her pension. Thank goodness for the 'Greenfly and Dandelions' blog she wrote for the Armstrong Newspaper Group website. At least no one else on the staff could write that.

And that was the good news.

All that expensive education notwithstanding, it was as good as a single mother without a degree, a single mother who had to put her child first could hope for. Even then she was luckier than most women in her situation. Luckier than she deserved according to her mother.

The bad news was that the *Observer* was cutting back on staff and a single mother with childcare issues was going to be top of the chop list.

'All done?' Hal unhooked a couple of mugs from the dresser, keeping an eye on Claire while he filled a bowl with warm water. Despite her insistence that she was fine, she was deathly pale.

'All done,' she said.

'You don't have to call the Town Hall and make your apologies?'

'No need.' She looked at the phone she was still

holding, then put it on the table. 'The news editor is handling it.'

'Right, well I'll clean up your foot.'

She frowned as he placed the bowl of water at her feet, then she rallied; he could practically hear her spine snapping straight. 'There's no need to make a fuss. I'll get in the shower as soon as you've gone.'

'It's cut,' he said. 'There's blood on the floor.'

'Is there?' She looked down and saw the trail of muddy, bloody footprints on her clean floor. 'Oh...' She bit back the word she'd undoubtedly have let drop if she'd been on her own. 'It must have been when I stepped on a stone.'

One sharp enough to cut her and yet she hadn't so much as whimpered. His fault. If he hadn't kissed her, if he'd just scraped the mud off her shoe, let her go...

'It might have been a piece of glass,' he said, not wanting to think about that kiss. About the button she'd been playing with or how she'd felt as she'd leaned against him as he'd helped her home. 'Or a ring pull from a can. I can't believe the litter down there.'

'A lot of it blows in from the towpath. It used to drive my dad wild.'

'It wasn't just me, then.' Before she could answer, he said, 'Stick your foot in this and soak off the dirt so that I can make sure there's nothing still in there.' She didn't bother to argue, just sucked in her breath as she lifted her foot into the water.

'Okay?'

She held her breath for a moment, then relaxed. 'Yes…'

He nodded and left her to soak while he made tea, adding a load of sugar to hers. Adding rather more than usual to his own.

He shouldn't have come to Cranbrook. He hadn't intended to come here. Not now. Not until it was all done. It had been his intention to keep his distance and leave it all to the consultants he'd engaged, but it was like a bad tooth you couldn't leave alone…

'Have you got any antiseptic?' he asked, setting the mug beside her.

'Under the sink, with the first-aid box.'

'Towel?'

'There's a clean one in the airing cupboard. It's in the bathroom at the top of the…'

'I know my way around.' He took a chocolate biscuit—it had been a long time since breakfast—and handed another to her. 'Eat this.'

'I—'

'It's medicinal,' he said, cutting off her objection, opening the door to stairs that seemed narrower than he remembered. He glanced back. 'You might want to lose the tights while I'm fetching it.'

'Are you quite sure I can manage that all by myself?'

He paused, his foot on the bottom step, and looked back. 'You have a mouth that will get you into serious trouble one of these days, Claire Thackeray.'

'Too late,' she said. 'It already has.'

'It's not a one-time-only option,' he pointed out and as she blushed virgin pink, he very nearly stepped back down into the kitchen to offer her a demonstration.

Peeling down tights over long, shapely legs that he'd already enjoyed at his leisure as she'd lain sprawled on top of him with her skirt around her waist would have offered some compensation in a day that was not, so far, going to plan.

He'd arrived at sunrise and set out for a quiet drive around the estate, wanting to claim its acres for himself. To enjoy his triumph.

The rush of possessiveness, unreasoning anger, when he'd seen a lad fishing from what had once been his favourite spot had brought him up short. Or maybe it had been the fancy rod and antique reel wielded so inexpertly that had irritated him. The boy had sworn it had belonged to his grand-dad, but he was very much afraid that it had been stolen.

Not the most pleasant start to the day and, once the boy had gone, he'd stopped to look, remembering his own wild days.

That's when he'd noticed that the bank opposite had been seriously undermined by the torrential winter rain. He'd pulled on the overalls and boots that had been lying in the back of the Land Rover and crossed the stream to take a closer look at the damage and walked right into the Claire and Archie double-act.

And if it hadn't been part of his plans to come back to Cranbrook Park until he'd made it his own, that was doubly so with Primrose Cottage.

There had been no reason to come down a lane on the edge of the village, a lane that stopped at a cottage that was hidden unless you were looking for it. Forgotten by the estate.

Jack North had never been prepared to use good drinking and gambling money to decorate, repair a house he did not own and Robert Cranbrook would have seen it fall down before he'd have allowed his workmen to touch it.

He never could understand why his mother had stayed. Some twisted sense of loyalty? Or was it guilt?

In his head the cottage had remained the way it had looked on the day he'd fired up his motorbike and ridden away. But, like him, it had changed out of all recognition.

The small window panes broken in one of Jack's drunken rages and stuffed with cardboard to keep out the weather had all been replaced and polished to a shine. Windows and trim were now painted white and the dull, blistering green front door was a fresh primrose yellow to match the flowers that were blooming all along the verge in front of a white-painted picket fence.

There had always been primroses…

Weeds no longer grew through the gravel path that led around to the rear; the yard, once half an acre of rank weeds where he'd spent hours stripping down and rebuilding an old motorcycle, was now a garden.

Inside everything had changed, too. His mother had battled against all odds to keep the place spotless. Now the walls had been stripped of the old wallpaper and painted in pale colours, the treads of the stairs each carpeted with a neatly trimmed offcut.

He'd once known every creak, every dip to avoid when he wanted to creep out at night and he still instinctively avoided them as he took the second flight to revisit his past.

Everything was changed up there, too.

Where he'd once stuck posters of motorcycles against the shabby attic walls, delicate little fairies now flitted across ivory wallpaper.

Did Claire Thackeray's little girl resemble her mother? All fair plaits and starched school uniform. Or did she betray her father?

He shook his head as if to clear the image. What Claire Thackeray had got up to and with whom, was none of his business.

None of this—the clean walls, stripped and polished floors, the pretty lace curtains—changed a thing. Taking it from her, doing to her what her father had done to him would be all the sweeter because the cottage was now something worth losing.

A towel…

The door to the front bedroom was shut and he didn't open it. Claire was disturbing enough without acquainting himself with the intimacy of her bedroom, but the back bedroom door stood wide open and he could see that it had been converted into an office.

An old wallpaper pasting table, painted dark green, served as a desk. On it there was an old laptop, a printer, a pile of books. Drawn to take a closer look, he found himself looking out of the window, down into the garden.

He'd hadn't been able to miss the fact that it was now a garden, rather than the neglected patch of earth he remembered, but from above he could see that it was a lot more.

Linked by winding paths, the ugly patch had been divided into a series of intimate spaces. Divided with trees and shrubs as herbaceous borders, there were places to sit, places to play and, at the rear, the kind of vegetable garden usually only seen on television programmes was tucked beneath the shelter of a bank on which spring bulbs were now dying back.

He looked down at the piles of books. He'd expected a thesaurus, a dictionary, whatever reference works journalists used. Instead, he found himself looking at a book on propagation. The other books were on greenhouse care, garden design.

Claire had done this?

Not without help. The house was decorated to a professional standard and the garden was immaculate.

He'd suggested that she was still all buttoned-up but her response to his kiss had blown that idea right out of the water. The woman Claire Thackeray had become would always have help.

He replaced the books, but as he turned away wanting to get out of this room, he was confronted by a cork board, thick with photographs of a little girl from babyhood to the most recent school photograph.

Her hair was jet black, and her golden skin was not the result of lying in the sun. Only her solemn grey eyes featured Claire and he could easily imagine the thrilling shock that must have run around the village when she'd wheeled her buggy into the village shop for the first time.

CHAPTER FOUR

'DID you have a good look round?' Claire asked, as he stepped down into the kitchen.

'I thought I'd better give you time to make yourself respectable,' he said, not bothering to deny it. 'It's all changed up there.'

It had changed everywhere.

Colour had begun to seep back into her cheeks and she raised a wry smile. 'Are you telling me that the young Hal North wasn't into "Forest Fairies"?'

'It wouldn't have mattered if I was,' he said. 'This house wasn't on the estate-maintenance rota and nothing would have persuaded Jack North to waste good drinking money on wallpaper.'

'I thought the cabbage roses in the front bedroom looked a bit pre-war,' she said. 'Not that I'm complaining. It was so old that it came off as easy as peeling a Christmas Satsuma.'

'You did it yourself?'

'That's what DIY stands for,' she said. 'I couldn't afford to pay someone to do it for me.'

'I didn't mean to sound patronising—'

She tutted. 'You missed. By a mile.'

'—but it's your landlord's job to keep the place in good repair.'

'Really? It didn't seem to work for your mother. In her shoes I'd have bought a few cans of paint and had a go myself.'

'She wouldn't…'

Hal's eyes were dark blue, she realised, with a fan of lines around them just waiting for him to smile. That bitten off "wouldn't," the snapping shut of his jaws, the hard line of his mouth, suggested that it wasn't going to happen if she gave way to her curiosity and asked him why a fit, handsome woman would choose to live like that.

'Sir Robert would only let me have the cottage on a repairing lease.'

'Cheapskate.'

'There was no money for renovations,' she said, leaping to his defence.

'So he got you to do it for him.'

'I had nowhere to live. He was doing me a favour.'

The cleaning, decorating, making a home for herself and Ally had kept her focussed, given her a purpose in those early months when her life had changed out of all recognition. No university, no job, no family. Just her and a new baby.

Cleaning, stripping, painting, making a home for them both had helped to keep the fear at bay.

'We both got a good deal, Hal. If the cottage had been fixed up, I couldn't have afforded the rent. He did get the materials for me at trade,' she said, 'and he replaced the broken glass and gutters himself.'

'Why am I not surprised?'

'I don't know,' she asked. 'Why aren't you?'

He shook his head. 'Are you ticklish?'

'What? No… What are you doing?' she demanded, confused by the sudden change in subject.

He didn't bother to answer but got down on one knee, soaped up his hands and picked up her foot.

She drew in a sharp breath as he smoothed his hand over her heel. 'Does that hurt?'

'It stings a bit.'

She lied.

With his fingers sliding over the arch of her foot, around her ankle, she was feeling no pain.

'Ally has started moaning about the wallpaper in her room,' she said, doing a swift subject change on her own account in a vain attempt to distract herself from the shimmer of pleasure rippling through her, an almost forgotten touch-me heaviness in her breasts, melting heat between her legs.

'Ally?'

'Alice Louise,' she said. 'After her grandmother.'

'Oh, right,' he said, and she knew he'd seen the photographs, put his own interpretation on her daughter's name.

'Apparently she's grown out of the fairy stage. It's hard to believe that she'll soon be eight.'

'Is eight too big for fairies?'

'Sadly.'

'So, what comes next?' She was mesmerised by the sight, the feel of his long fingers as they carefully teased the grit from between her toes. They were covered with small scars, the kind you got from knocks, scrapes, contact with hot metal. A mechanic's hands... 'Ballet?' he asked, looking up, catching her staring. 'Horses?'

'Not ballet,' she said quickly. 'She loves horses, but I can't afford to indulge her. To be honest, I don't care what she chooses, just as long as there is a stage between now and boys. They grow up so quickly these days.'

'They always did, Claire.'

'Did they? I must have missed that stage. Too much homework, I suppose.' And not enough freedom to hang around the village, giggling with the other girls, dressed to attract the boys. Not that they'd have welcomed her. The girls, anyway. She'd received sideways looks from the boys, but no one had been brave enough to make a move… 'The local girls my age seemed so much more grown up.' So much more knowing.

'You appear to have caught up.'

She shook her head. 'You never get that back.' She'd still been hopelessly naïve at eighteen, believing sex and love were the same thing. Not wanting to think about that, she said, 'I'm taking Ally to the DIY store at the weekend to look around, see what catches her eye.'

'Shouldn't you wait and see what the new owner has in mind before you part with more hard cash on a house you don't own?'

'A few rolls of wallpaper won't break the bank.' And decorating would keep her mind off it. 'When he sees what a great tenant I am,' she added, 'he'll probably beg me to stay.'

He didn't comment, but instead turned another chair to face her, covered it with a towel and rested her dripping foot on it.

'Shouldn't you be at work?' she asked, as he tipped the dirty water down the sink and rinsed the bowl before refilling it with clean water to which he added antiseptic. Anything to stop thinking about the way his hands had felt on her foot, her ankle. How good it felt to be cared for.

The big hole that was missing not just from Ally's life, but her own.

'Not until I've dealt with this,' he said, washing her foot again, but this time when he lifted it up, he sat on the chair and set both towel and foot on his knee so that he could take a closer look at the damage.

It was one of those 'clean knicker' moments—except for clean knickers substitute nail polish.

'Never go out without painting your toenails in case you have an accident and some good-looking man decides to wash your foot...'

Who knew?

'No glass, it's just a nasty little cut,' he said, patting the heel dry before working the towel through her toes. She was really regretting the lack of nail polish... 'If you'll hand me a dressing?' he prompted.

She tore the cover off a big square dressing and handed it to him, shivering slightly as his fingers brushed against hers.

'You're cold. Drink your tea,' he said, as he

placed the dressing over the cut, smoothed it into place and continued to hold her foot.

'It's too sweet,' she said, shuddering as she took a sip.

'Think of it as medicine,' he said as the phone in his pocket began to ring. He glanced at it. 'I have to go,' he said, without bothering to answer it, transferring her foot from his knee to the chair as he stood up. 'Keep an eye on that. Any redness, don't hang about, straight to the surgery for some antibiotics.'

'Yes, doc.'

He picked up the bowl, emptied it in the sink, dried his hands and was gone.

'Thank you, doc,' she said to herself, and the sound of his footsteps crunching on the gravel grew fainter and the silence returned.

She didn't move.

While she hadn't used her imagination in a long while, it was, apparently, still in full working order and if she kept still, concentrated very hard, she could still feel his hands on her foot, the sensual slide of his fingers between her toes.

Claire had just stepped out of the shower when a rap at the door sent her heart racing.

'Claire? It's Pen.'

Not Hal with her bike, her shoe, but a neighbour. She opened the window and called down, 'Hold on, Penny, I'll be right there.'

She threw on a sweatshirt, wincing as her shoulder reminded her that it, too, had been in the wars, and a pair of comfortable jeans.

'Are you all right?' Pen watched her limp across to the kettle and switch it on. 'I was in the village shop and Mrs Judd said she saw some man helping you home.'

Life in Cranbrook might have changed out of all recognition in the last decade but the impossibility of doing anything without everyone knowing in ten minutes flat remained a constant. Which meant that Hal North couldn't be living in the village. He wasn't a man you would miss when he pitched up in your neighbourhood and Penny, who was always urging her to get out and find someone, would have been full of it.

'Earth to Claire…'

'Sorry, Pen. I fell off my bike.'

'I wonder who he was?' Penny said, ten minutes later when, hands clutched tightly around a warm mug, she'd heard the severely edited highlights of her accident.

'You haven't taken on anyone new?' Claire asked. 'I hear the estate has been sold.'

'Who told you that?' she demanded. 'It's not being announced until Monday.'

'So who's bought the place? Don't worry, I won't say a word before it's official. I just want a chance to dig up some background details.'

Something to add a bit of sparkle to the two-page spread of the history of the house and the Cranbrook family that she'd been working on since it was evident that the estate would have to be sold. Without some background on the new owners, it was just that. History.

'Well…' Penny stretched the word like a piece of elastic as she helped herself to a chocolate-chip cookie and propped her elbows on the table. 'According to the solicitors' clerk it's been bought by a millionaire businessman.'

'Well, yes. Obviously.' Who else could afford it? 'He'll need millions if he's going to live there.' Spend millions to bring it up to modern specifications. That had to be good news for the local economy. 'What kind of business, do you know? Is he married? Does he have children?' They were the details that the *Observer* readers would want.

'Sorry, but I did have a call from a Ms Beatrice

Webb this morning, who wants to discuss my future with the estate on Monday.'

A woman? Well, why not…

'I should have asked for more information but to be honest I was too shocked to do anything other than say I'd be there.'

Claire curbed her impatience. 'That sounds hopeful.'

'Does it? With Steve on short time and Gary without a hope of a job, my few hours in the estate office and the money you give me for taking care of Ally after school is all that's keeping us afloat at the moment.'

'The estate will still need managing, Penny. The new owner, whoever he or she is, is going to need you.' She didn't mention her appeal to Hal on Gary's behalf. No point in raising false hopes.

Penny pulled a face. 'Ms Webb sounded capable of running the whole shebang with one hand tied behind her back.'

'She's probably got more than enough work to keep her busy in London.'

'London?'

'I imagine that's where the millions are made. A country estate is a plaything. A weekend retreat,' she added.

If Ms Webb planned to use it to hold shooting and fishing parties for business contacts she'd need someone who knew what he was doing to run the place. Take care of the game birds, the trout stocks.

Someone like Hal.

A tiny flutter of anticipation invaded her stomach and she grabbed a chocolate-chip cookie in an effort to smother it. The man was a menace and she had enough on her plate without getting involved.

Involved! That was a joke. Hal North was never going to be interested in a buttoned-up woman with a sharp tongue. The hot imprint of his lips on hers meant nothing.

'The rumour in the post office on Monday was that it's going to be converted into a hotel and conference centre,' Penny said.

'There are all kinds of rumours flying around,' Claire said, 'but that wouldn't be such a bad thing and you have to admit that the Hall has got everything going for it. The location is stunning and there's probably room for a golf course on the other side of the Cran.'

'Really? How much room does a golf course take?'

She grinned. 'I've no idea, but look on the bright side. Whatever the future, a new owner means that there's going to be work for local builders, crafts-men, grounds men and that has to mean work for Steve.'

'Maybe Gary, too,' Penny said, cheered. 'There might even be more hours for me.'

'Absolutely.' Then, as casually as she could, she asked, 'Is Gary at home today?'

'According to him it's a study day although the only thing he's studying is how to cast a fly.'

Which answered that question. 'Well, if he could spare the time, I wonder if he'd pick up my bike for me. It's still on the footpath.'

'When he comes home to raid the fridge I'll ask him.'

The minute she'd shut the door on her Claire picked up the phone and dialled the number for the Hall.

'Cranbrook Hall.'

The unfamiliar voice was rich and plummy. 'Miss Webb?' On being assured that it was, she said, 'Welcome to Cranbrook Park. I'm Claire Thackeray—'

'Yes?'

No 'how can I help you?' No easy way in.

'—from the *Maybridge Observer.* I understand that Cranbrook Park has a new owner,' she said, pausing briefly. Nothing. 'As you can imagine, there are all kinds of rumours flying around at the moment and, inevitably, there are concerns about jobs.' The few that there were. 'The hope that if the Park is going to be developed commercially there will be work for local people,' she prompted.

Still no response.

'There has always been a very close relationship between the town and estate,' she continued, despite the lack of encouragement. 'Charity events, that sort of thing?' Good grief, this was like drawing blood from a very dry stone. 'I wondered if you could spare me half an hour to talk about the future of the estate? Maybe fill in some background detail for our readers?' she added hopefully.

'Don't you people talk to one another?' she replied, impatiently. 'Your editor called half an hour ago and I told him what I'll tell you. Mr North does not speak to the press.'

Ouch.

'I'm sorry, I haven't been in the office this morning and while the editor would be looking for facts, something to fill in the gaps in the announcement about the sale, I'm more interested in the human-interest angle. As I said the Park is a big part of the local community...'

And then the name sank in.

North.

No. She must have misheard. Or it was a coincidence. There was another North. It couldn't be…

'Did you say North?' she asked.

'Ask your editor, Miss Thackeray. He has all the details that are being released to the press.'

'Yes… Thank you,' she added belatedly as the dialling tone kicked in.

No…

No, no, no, no, no…

She repeated the word with every step as she ran upstairs to the office and turned on her cranky laptop. Kept saying it as it took an age to boot up. Even as she searched on the internet for Hal…no, Henry North.

It. Could. Not. Be. Him.

There was no shortage of hits—there were, apparently, a lot of Henry Norths in the world—and rather than plough through them, she switched to 'images' to see if she recognised any of them.

There were dozens of photographs, but one leapt out at her and it was the shock of seeing Hal face to face in the ditch all over again. That stop-the-world total loss of breath where the only thing moving was her mind, and that was spinning like a top. Seeing it in front of her she refused to believe it even when she clicked on the image to bring up the document it was attached to; a company report.

She knew it couldn't be true. But there he was. Hal North. In full colour.

The Hal North she'd knocked off his feet a couple of hours ago was, apparently, the Henry North who owned a freight company. Make that an international freight company.

The one with the sleek black-and-silver HALGO livery familiar to anyone who'd ever stood at a bus stop by a busy road watching the traffic thunder by.

Vans, trucks, eighteen-wheelers, not to mention air cargo and shipping.

Hal North, her Hal North, was the chairman of a household-name company with a turnover in billions.

'Hal! At last. Where on earth have you been?' Bea Webb rarely got agitated, but she was agitated now. 'I've organised the staff meetings for Monday, but I have to get back to London and so do you.'

'Sorry. I was looking around the Park and got sidetracked.'

'Collecting junk left by fly-tippers more like,'

she said, as he lifted Claire's bike off the back of a Land Rover.

'I couldn't just leave it there,' he said. Easier than telling her what had really happened.

'Well, don't. The consultants have arranged for a contractor to come in and do a thorough clean-up of the estate, clear the outbuildings. Do you want me to organise someone to take a look through all this junk before they start?' she asked, with a dismissive wave in the direction of the ornate, eighteenth-century stable block. 'Just in case there's a priceless Chinese vase tucked away in a box of discarded china?'

'Don't bother,' he said. 'Cranbrook had experts go through it all with a fine-tooth comb in the hopes of finding buried treasure.' Anything to save him bankruptcy. Anything to save him from being forced by his creditors to sell to him.

It was knowing that Sir Robert Cranbrook wouldn't see a penny of his money that had made paying the price almost a pleasure. Once the tax man had taken his cut, the remainder would go to the estate's creditors; the small people Cranbrook had never given a damn about so long as he continued to live in luxury.

That and the fact that Robert Cranbrook knew

that every moment of comfort left to him was being paid for by the son he'd never wanted. Whom he'd always refused to acknowledge. Knowing how much he'd hate that, but not having the moral fibre to tell him to go to hell, was the sweetest revenge.

'What I do need is a front loader. The public footpath running beside the stream has been seriously undermined and is in danger of collapse. We can use some of this stuff to make a temporary barrier. The last thing I need is for someone to get hurt.'

'Terrific,' she said. 'Tell me again why you bought this place?'

'The Cran is a great trout stream. I thought I'd take up fishing,' he said, removing Gary Harker's rod from the back of the Land Rover.

Her eyebrows suggested she was not convinced, but she confined herself to, 'Not today. You've got a board meeting at two-thirty and if we don't get moving you'll be late.'

'I gave Angus a call and asked him to stand in for me.' Her eyebrows rose a notch. 'He can handle it and right now I'm needed here.'

'In other words you want to play with your expensive new toy.'

'Every man needs a hobby.'

'Renting a stretch of someone else's trout stream would have been a lot cheaper,' she pointed out. 'Besides, I thought you were going to leave all this to the experts. Keep a low profile.'

'This is the country. No chance of that.' Not when you'd just had a close encounter with the local press. 'Front loaders?' he prompted, picking up Claire's bike then, as Bea called up an app on her phone to search for a local hire company. 'Any messages?'

She shook her head, then looked up. 'Were you expecting a call?'

'No.' As far as Claire knew there was no one to take a complaint about uppity staff who took shocking advantage of maidens in distress. On the other hand... 'I thought you might have heard from the local paper.'

'No "might" about it. The editor rang, hoping for a quote to go with the announcement of the sale they're running in Monday's edition. Then there was some girl wanting "the personal angle" on the new owner of Cranbrook Park...' Her phone began to ring. 'Don't worry, Hal. I made it clear that you don't give interviews.'

Some girl.

No prizes for guessing who that was. Claire

Thackeray hadn't been so shocked by her tumble, by her confrontation with him, that she'd neglected to follow up the news that the estate had been sold.

'Hold on, Katie…' She held the phone to her chest. 'Is there anything else, only I really do need to get home. There's an open evening at Katie's school this evening.'

'Don't worry. I've got it covered.' He picked up the bike. 'Tell Katie that she can come down for the half term if she likes. She'll enjoy the deer.

'You're staying down here?' she asked.

'For a week. Maybe two. The roof needs immediate attention. It's getting me out of the office,' he pointed out, when she would have protested. 'Something you're always encouraging.'

'Creating barriers for footpaths and dealing with a leaky roof wasn't quite what I had in mind. And thanks for the invitation but we're headed to Italy and guaranteed sunshine. Lying by the pool beats picking up rubbish hands down. There's plenty of space if you fancy a change of scene,' she said.

'I'll think about it,' he said, but they both knew he wouldn't. Travel was something he did because he had to, for business. Right now all he wanted to do was get on his Harley and ride around the estate the way he used to, although it wouldn't be as much fun without some furious gardener or game-keeper chasing him on a quad bike.

Nothing was as much fun these days.

He blocked out Robert Cranbrook's mocking voice, and looked around. He had more than enough to get out of bed for. Everything was shabby, worn out. There were weeds growing out of what had once been perfectly raked gravel, and water stains on the walls where broken guttering hadn't been repaired.

When he was a kid this had been gleaming, cared for. A place where only the privileged few—and their staff—were allowed. Forbidden territory for the likes of him. Not that he'd taken any notice of that.

Ignoring the rules, going where he wasn't allowed, dodging the staff to explore the seemingly endless empty rooms had been a challenge.

He'd never taken anything, not even as much as a polished apple from a bowl; he'd simply wanted to tread the centuries-old floors, finger the linen-fold panels, look at the paintings, absorb the history that he'd been denied as he'd wandered through the empty, unused rooms.

There had been a moment of elation, triumph when he'd picked up the deeds and tossed them casually to his company lawyer that even Robert Cranbrook's outburst couldn't sour. But while he was now the proud owner of the Hall with its leaking roof and crumbling fences, ironically, the only place on the estate where the paintwork was glossy and well cared for was the house he'd once lived in.

And it was Claire Thackeray's unexpected response to his ill-advised kiss that was burning a hole in his brain; the memory of her slim foot, her ankle resting in his hands, playing havoc with his senses.

CHAPTER FIVE

CLAIRE stared at the screen.

Hal North had been turned off the estate by Sir Robert with nothing to his name but a motorbike and a bad attitude on his nineteenth birthday. Now he was back, the chairman of an international company. A millionaire. A millionaire she'd accused of fishing without a licence. A millionaire to whom she'd offered her last ten-pound note.

He must be laughing fit to bust.

Well, let him laugh, she thought, as she clicked furiously on the links, determined to find out all she could about where he'd been, what he'd been doing since he left. How he'd made his money.

She'd teach Hal North to make sarcastic comments about working for a local paper.

Human interest?

This was human interest in letters ten feet high. A story that she could write because she'd been there at the beginning. One that she knew hadn't been told because it would have been a sensation in Cranbrook. A sensation in Maybridge.

Headline material.

Prodigal returns, buys up the big house and has hot, sweaty sex with the girl he left behind...

Whoa, whoa!

She didn't write fantasy, she dealt in reality.

And she didn't write gossip. She had been told to stay at home for the rest of the week and she'd use the time to get ahead on the G&D blog.

She was taking photographs of a particularly large slug—planning a piece on organic control—when her phone rang.

She took it out of her pocket, checked the caller. So much for putting her feet up...

'Hello, Brian,' she said.

'Claire... How are you feeling now?' he asked, all sympathy.

Having insisted that she was ready to come into work, she could hardly say she was hors d'combat. Not that he waited for an answer.

'Any chance you could do a bit of research on the new owner of Cranbrook Park? Nothing you'll have to leave the house for.'

Yes, well, she was the one who'd insisted that the Park was her territory.

'What do you want to know?'

'General background. Where he comes from, family, that sort of thing. I'll send you what we've got. Unless it's too much trouble?' he added, apparently picking up on her lack of enthusiasm.

'No, no, of course not. I was using the down time to catch up on my gardening blog, but it can wait.'

'Good girl.'

'Patronising oaf,' she muttered, but only when he'd hung up.

Back in her office, she checked her email and, just in case she was in any doubt, there was the press release, embargoed until Monday, telling the world that Henry North had bought Cranbrook Park.

The moment it emerged he was local—and there would be plenty of people who remembered him—it would become obvious to Brian that she would have known him. He'd want specifics, details.

She opened up a new document and began to makes notes. Everything she knew about Hal. His parents, school.

She fired off an email to the recently retired headmistress of the village school to get a quote, called Maybridge High and spoke to the school secretary who pointed her in the direction of teachers who would remember him. She left messages for them to call her back. That done, she hit the internet in order to find out what he'd been up to since he'd left Cranbrook. How he'd transformed himself from disaffected youth to millionaire. That was the big story.

She ran into a blank wall.

When Ms Webb said that Mr North did not speak to the press, she hadn't been kidding.

Hal wasn't one of those CEOs who courted publicity. He didn't date supermodels, big himself up on television talk shows, or appear in *Celebrity* magazine attending showbiz parties. Of course he didn't. If he'd done any of those things she would, undoubtedly, have seen him. And if he was happily married with a parcel of children he'd kept that to himself, as well.

The kiss that still burned on her lips suggested otherwise. Or, if he was married, the relationship was clearly more of a hobby than a full-time occupation.

No.

Despite the endless stream of girls who had made his life sweet when he was a youth living on the estate, she didn't see him as a man who'd play the field once he'd found his mate.

'Oh, get real,' she muttered.

She knew nothing about him. Only that he made the air sizzle. Made her pulse race, her heart pound. Which was as ridiculous now as it had been when she was a pre-pubescent fantasist who would have fainted if he'd as much as winked at her.

Okay. She had the boy, the youth and by the time she left to pick up Ally from school, she had school photographs, anecdotes from teachers and enough general background to email Brian and ask him if she could go to London on a quest to fill in the more recent past. The fact that he agreed so readily, suggested he had already drawn a blank himself.

She'd just opened the back door when she heard the crunch of gravel. Gary with her bike.

Not Gary.

Like iron filings, a gazillion cells turned in one direction as if someone had switched on an electro-magnet. That had to explain the sudden dizziness as Hal North rounded the corner of the cottage, stopped as he saw her.

'You're on your way out?' he asked.

'I was just going to pick up Ally from school,' she said, banging the door behind her and heading for the gate.

'How's your foot?' he asked, falling in beside her.

'What? Oh, good as new,' she said. Not. Her heel was throbbing and walking on the gravel was painful. 'What do you want, Hal?'

'To explain about your bike.' He looked at her foot, clearly not convinced. 'Can I give you a lift? We can talk on the way.'

There was an ancient estate Land Rover parked at the gate and he opened the door. It was high and as she put her weight on her foot to haul herself up, she gave a little gasp and he put his hands on her backside and gave her a boost up.

'Okay?'

Okay?

You went eight years without a man's hand on your backside and then it happened twice in as many days...

'Fine,' she snapped and reached to the seat belt, any excuse to look away.

He climbed in beside her, teased the cranky old machine into life, then turned it and headed into the village.

'So? What's the verdict on my bike?' she asked.

'It's a mess,' he said, above the noise of the engine. 'You're going to need a new wheel and front mudguard. I'm doing my best to locate one.'

'You could have phoned to tell me that.' Then, aware that she had sounded less than grateful, 'I meant you didn't have to come specially.'

'I was at this end of the estate.'

'Inspecting your domain?'

He glanced at her. 'Something like that,' he said.

Damn! There were a hundred questions she wanted to ask and she'd blown her chance with a snarky remark. But while it was easy enough to be focussed, professional when he was just a name, a face on her computer, up close and personal—with the imprint of his hand on her bottom still warm in the memory—it was difficult to be dispassionate. Professional. Cool.

'When were you going to tell me that you've bought Cranbrook Park?' she asked, doing her best to recover the situation.

'Would you have believed me if I'd told you this morning?'

'We'll never know,' she said, as he pulled up in front the school. Then, rolling her eyes she said, 'Probably not.'

'No.' Her honesty earned her one of those rare smiles. 'And I knew you'd read about it in the paper on Monday.'

A group of mothers turned as one to see who had arrived. Gossip city.

'I'd better go. I'm supposed to be supervising some workmen.'

'You're going to be a hands-on lord of the manor, then?' It had been a very long time since she'd given anyone anything to talk about so she might as well make the most of it.

'Just taking a few days out to play with my expensive new toy,' he said, with the merest edge of self-mockery in response to her sarcasm.

'Expensive, I have no doubt, but Cranbrook Park is not a toy.'

'No. Like all my investments, it will have to work for its keep.'

'How? What are you going to do with it?'

He leaned across her, threatening a sensory overload as his arm came within a whisker of her breast and she had a close-up of his cheekbone, a lungful of the scent of his skin, hair as he opened her door. 'I'll have someone bring your bike back when it's fixed.'

She slid down onto the pavement, turned to face him.

'Ask Gary,' she said. 'He might even be able to

straighten out the wheel. He's like you, good with his hands.' And she blushed.

'Goodbye, Claire.'

'Goodbye, Hal. Thanks for the lift.'

She slammed the door shut and watched the old Land Rover move away through the village leaving her engulfed in the scent of hot metal and diesel.

Work for its keep...

Was that a warning that her days of paying a low rent in return for keeping the cottage in good repair were running out?

He'd warned her not to spend money on wallpaper...

All her hard work would mean nothing to him. Her cottage was pretty, her garden was a showpiece. It would fetch three times the rent she paid on the open market.

It wasn't just her job that was under threat, but she was being forced to seriously consider the possibility that she would lose her home.

'Mum!' Ally flung herself at her.

'Hi, angel. I'm home early so I thought I'd come and meet you. Do you want to ask Savannah if she'd like to come to tea?'

'Absolutely not. I am never talking to her again.'

Oh, terrific.

* * *

He could have phoned, should have phoned, Hal knew, but like coming back to Cranbrook Park, he was drawn to Claire Thackeray by something he couldn't explain.

Robert Cranbrook was right, he had obsessed about owning the Park, it had driven him and he'd commissioned plans for its future long before it had been on the market. He'd known it was only a matter of time.

It had all seemed so simple; what he'd do, how it would feel but then, this morning, he'd seen that boy—so like himself at that age. No respect. Full of what the world owed him. It had been like a kick in the gut.

And then he'd been run down by the Claire and Archie double act and the kick had been physical rather than metaphorical.

Local Boy Saves Cranbrook Park

Solicitors acting for Sir Robert Cranbrook announced this morning that the Cranbrook Park estate has been sold to millionaire businessman, Henry North.

For Mr North, founder and CEO of HALGO, the international freight company, this is a very special homecoming. Born in Maybridge, both his parents worked for Sir Robert Cranbrook and he went to both Cranbrook Primary and Maybridge High Schools before leaving the area to set up his own business.

Mrs Mary Bridges, retired Head Teacher of Cranbrook Primary School remembers Mr North well, describing him as 'full of life' and he's remembered at Maybridge High School as a promising student who, even as a youth, demonstrated a well-honed entrepreneurial spirit.

Former residents of the estate recall that he was a keen fisherman and he will no doubt take full advantage of the excellent fishing in the famous trout stream for which the Park is named.

Henry North started his own motorcycle courier service upon leaving school and he swiftly fulfilled his early promise, rapidly expanding his business to compete with major freight companies at home and internationally. When his company was floated on the stock exchange three years ago, his personal fortune was estimated to be in nine figures.

Rumours have been flying around all week, suggesting that the estate will be transformed into a leisure facility but Mr North, 33, divorced, is keeping his plans for the estate under wraps for the moment. He did however confirm that it would, like all his investments, have to 'work for its keep,' which sounds promising for local jobs.

—*Maybridge Observer,* Monday April 24

'Excellent job, Claire.' Brian leaned back in his chair. 'Obviously we went to the internet, but it was pretty thin considering who he is and we missed the local connection. Of course you live on the estate. Did you know him?'

'He's a bit older than me,' she said.

'Of course. You must have been just a kid when he left. You did well to get hold of the school photographs so quickly.'

'Thanks.' She handed him her expense sheet for Friday. Her fare—cheap day return, receipts for copies of his birth, marriage and divorce certificates, as well her lunch in the café near his office.

She'd felt like a proper reporter as she'd struck up a conversation with the girl clearing the tables, pretending that she'd been offered a job with the company. As she'd hoped, most of his staff ate there at lunchtime and, no surprise, the women talked about their good-looking, eligible boss.

'I kept my expenses to the bare minimum,' she

said, as his eyebrows rose at the amount. 'Worth it simply for the information that he's unattached, I'd say. How many copies is a front-page photograph of a good-looking, eligible millionaire in the neighbourhood going to be worth?'

'I don't know.'

'Women buy the local newspaper,' she pointed out.

'True, but how often can we use him on the front page? Until we know what his plans are he's not going to be headline news.'

'You don't need headline news. I'll give you stories,' she promised. 'All you need on the front page is a photograph and a caption leading on to page two. It's how they use the royal family to sell papers.'

'Shame he doesn't have a title to go with all that money, but you can't have everything.' He grinned, signed the sheet and handed it back to her. 'With the way circulation is falling, anything is worth a try, but no more trips to London.'

The phone rang once, twice, three times. He checked his watch. Ten on the dot.

He picked up the receiver, sat back in the leather

chair worn smooth by generations of Cranbrook men. 'What do you want, Claire?'

'And good morning to you, Hal.'

'Is it good? I hadn't noticed.'

'Shame on you. I was earthing-up my potatoes as the sun rose with a robin for company.'

He was at his desk dealing with the reports and emails that, these days, seemed to multiply faster than he could deal with.

'I hope you weren't late for work again.'

'I was, but only because the bus was late. Any news on my bike?'

'I'll chase it up. If that's all?' he prompted, knowing full well it wasn't.

'How about an update on your plans for the future of Cranbrook Park?' she asked, in a clear, bright musical voice that was inextricably tied into a burning sense of injustice, of longing for something beyond his reach. Was Robert Cranbrook right? Was this the end rather than the beginning he'd envisaged? 'Just a little hint?' she prompted. 'Something I can use in tomorrow's paper?'

'It's none of your business?' he offered. That 'boy' in the *Observer*'s headline had been too reminiscent of Cranbrook's bile.

'No…I'm going to need more than that.'

Was she laughing?

'It's none of your business, Claire Thackeray?' he offered, restraining the urge to join her.

'Okay. We'll leave that for now but I was hoping you'd explain to our readers why you've blocked off the public footpath beside the Cran?'

'Do your readers care?' he asked. 'No one has complained.'

'Clearly you don't read our letters page.'

'I don't read the *Observer,*' he lied, 'but I have no doubt that "outraged of Maybridge" is an inside job.'

'How cynical you are. People do care.'

'No comment.'

'So that's a "no comment", a "no comment" and a "no comment," then. Okay,' she said—definitely laughing— 'That'll do nicely.'

'Claire… How's your foot?'

'I'm scarred for life. You'll be hearing from my lawyers any day now. How's your, um, rod?' she asked.

'I refer you to the answer I gave earlier.'

'It would make a great story. Millionaire Landowner Mown Down by Tenant. Archie has form, you know. He ran some quad bikers into the stream last year. I'll send you a link to the article.'

'You wouldn't rat on Archie,' he said, as an email popped into his inbox. 'How do you know my email address?'

'No comment and no comment. It's a good picture of him, don't you think?'

He clicked on the link, looked at the photograph of Archie, the picture of sweet innocence as he peered over the hedge.

'Believe nothing that you read and only half what you see,' he replied and thought he caught a sigh from the other end of the phone.

'Any progress with my bike?' she asked.

'Ask Gary. He's working on it.'

'I will and, Hal?'

'Yes?'

'Thanks for giving him a chance. The offer of a cake is still open. Any time.'

'Just stop ringing me and we'll be quits,' he said, hanging up before he relented.

The estimate for re-leading the roof dealt with the smile.

'Made the front page again, Claire?'

'Homing instinct,' she said, glancing at the pulls of the front page. The Maybridge Wish-List fairy might be draped over the masthead, but it was her story that was the lead. '"Closed for Fun..." It has a nice ring to it, don't you think?' she said, doing her best to sound enthusiastic.

'It was a slow news day.' Tim Mayhew, the sports editor, made a virtue of being a grouch.

'This is Maybridge, Tim. It's always a slow news day. The ambitious journalist has to get out there and create her headlines.'

That would be the journalist who was desperate to hang on to her job. The journalist who wished she hadn't promised the news editor a constant feed of Hal North stories.

'There's nothing wrong with ambition,' Tim said, 'but you're going to have to come up with something better than local landowner closes footpath if you're going to repeat your local-boy-makes-good coup.'

She didn't need him to tell her that. Brian was already on her case.

'It's not the footpath that makes the story, Tim, it's the "new," "millionaire" and "landowner" that does the business.' Along with the tall, dark. The classically handsome element was cancelled out by rich and available.

'People will soon get fed up of being fed a diet of Hal North stories.'

The sooner the better. She couldn't wait to get back to the WI meetings, meanwhile…

'I've just heard that he's cancelled the traditional Teddy Bears Picnic. Just who the heck does think he is?' she asked, trying to put some real feeling into it.

'Henry North? New millionaire landowner?' he said, quoting her own words back at her.

She stared at the front-page picture of the pile of scrap metal blocking the footpath across the Cranbrook estate.

The photographer had used a marker to write "Closed For Fun" on a piece of cardboard and propped it against a handy piece of junk. It made a great picture, she didn't deny it. And Brian had found a photograph of Hal at a white-tie dinner. The juxtaposition suggested arrogance, distance, a man who didn't care.

Tim grunted. 'Personally, I don't blame him for refusing to have dozens of kids running riot on his newly acquired country estate.'

'Next to you the Grinch is warm and cuddly.'

Hal wasn't like that.

She mentally rolled her eyes. She kept telling herself that 'Hal wasn't like that'; she hadn't a clue what he was like. All she had was this fantasy figure she'd created in her head—a cross between Prince Charming and the Beast. And if she'd cast herself in the role of Beauty, it was because she'd been a kid and didn't know any better.

What she did know was that it hadn't been 'Mr Henry North, millionaire businessman' who'd mocked her, reminded her that she had once had a goal in life. A place at a good university, every advantage, and she'd wasted it. And it sure as heck hadn't been 'Mr Henry North, millionaire businessman' who'd kissed her socks off. Well, her tights, anyway...

That had most definitely been Hal North, Cranbrook bad boy, doing what he did as naturally as breathing. She'd put his bad temper down to the fact that she'd run into him. That must have hurt. But having reinvented himself it must have come as quite a shock to discover that she was still on the estate and working for the local newspaper.

He'd got off lightly, she reminded herself.

She could have got a lot more quotes to liven up her original front page if she'd had a mind to, but she'd kept that to herself. She wasn't about to annoy the man who had it in his power to put up her rent.

'It's really tough on the charity that relies on the event,' she said. Concentrate on that. Not on Hal.

'It must have come as a real shock when Cranbrook Park was sold overnight to a man who doesn't buy into the whole noblesse-oblige thing.'

'It was quick, wasn't it?' Almost as if Hal had been watching, waiting…

'Once you're in hock to the tax man you're done for. They won't wait for the market to pick up. As long as they're covered they don't care how cheap they sell. And it would need to be cheap. The place is going to take a fortune to restore.'

'I suppose.'

'No doubt North will finance it with a high-end executive estate on that meadow running beside the May. It's a prime riverside location and out of sight of the Hall. Perfect.'

'What? But that's Archie's meadow!' she protested. He was right, though. It was perfect. Forget dancing on Sir Robert's grave. How much more satisfying would Hal find it to make Sir Robert watch as he trampolined a thousand years of Cranbrook family history into the dirt. 'He'd never get it through planning,' she objected.

'You think a man like North is going to let petty bureaucracy stand in his way? If the local planners prove obstinate, he'll put in a appeal to the Secretary of State on the grounds of the local need for jobs, houses.' He shrugged. 'They're probably mates. There's a story for you.'

'I can't print that!'

She wouldn't have to. All it would take was a photograph of them together and people would leap to their own conclusions. And there was nothing like a suggestion of dirty doings at the Town Hall to boost circulation.

She would be flavour of the month. And if it made her feel just a little bit soiled? The way she'd felt as she'd listened to gossip about him in the café near his office, well, it was her job. It paid the rent, kept Ally warm and fed.

'Besides, what will happen to poor old Archie?'

'Oh, please. If North has any sense that donkey was cats' meat within a week of him moving in. You should sue him for not keeping him under control,' he added. 'Or are you saving that for another headline?'

'Of course not. He's always been a lamb with me.' As long as she had an apple to buy him off. 'Archie,' she added, rubbing the back of her hand over her mouth. Hal North was something else…

'Kebabs, then. Millionaire Makes Mincemeat of Maybridge Mascot...'

'Shut up, Tim,' she muttered as Brian walked through the office.

'Children, children!' Jessica Dixon, the features editor raised her head from her PC. 'The only thing that should concern you on today's front page is who is going to be this year's Fairy Godmother. Or Godfather,' she added, looking at Tim over her spectacles. 'This is an equal-opportunity chance to volunteer.'

'Tim in a tutu and wings.' Cheered at the thought, Claire grinned. 'Now that I would pay good money to see.'

CHAPTER SIX

Maybridge wish week!

Iᴛ' s Maybridge Wish Week! Time for the *Maybridge Observer*'s Fairy Godmother to wave her magic wand and make some wishes come true for members of the community.

In the past few years, we've hunted down grant funding, drummed up support from local business and enlisted the help of a volunteer army from our community to refurbish the pensioners' day-care centre, built a modern, fully equipped sports pavilion on the old playing fields and turned a derelict cinema into an arts centre that is now a vibrant part of Maybridge life, as well as dozens of smaller projects to make life easier for groups and individuals.

So—what next?

We're asking you to tell us what project you'd like to see tackled this year…

—*Maybridge Observer,* April 27.

* * *

'Have you seen this?'

Hal glanced at the newspaper Bea Webb was holding up.

'The *Maybridge Observer* Fairy Godmother?' he asked blandly, ignoring the headline and concentrating instead on the cartoon fairy waving her wand and sprinkling gold sparkle over the newspaper masthead.

She looked exactly like Claire Thackeray.

'If only. According to this, Maybridge has become a "fun-free zone" since your arrival.'

He took the paper from her and dropped it in the bin, refusing to think about the way she called him every day at the same time to ask about his plans. To think about the fact that he was always at his desk, waiting for her call. Glancing at his watch if she was a little late.

That her voice, clear, confident, the product of all that expensive private education that had gone to waste in a moment of lust with a man who hadn't bothered to stick around and deal with his own mess, had taken up residence in his head.

'I need someone in the office full-time, Bea,' he said, firmly changing the subject. 'Will you ask Penny if she's prepared to do more hours?'

She shook her head. 'Why don't you stick to the plan and leave all this to the professionals, Hal?'

Good question.

Claire knew that Tim had just been winding her up, but she couldn't get Archie out of her head.

Okay, he was a bit—more than a bit—of a liability and while Sir Robert might have had a soft spot for the beast, Hal North had no reason to consider him anything but a pain in the fishing rod, but…

Just…but.

She looked up as Brian stopped by her desk. 'How far have you got with the Teddy Bears Picnic story, Claire?'

'I'm working on it,' she said. 'I thought I might run over and take some photographs of Cranbrook woods.'

'No need. I sent Marcus over there this morning. I want you to focus on the "all this and he won't share it for a day, not even for a good cause" angle.' Her heart was still sinking when he said, 'On the other hand, it wouldn't hurt to go and have a good look round. Take some pictures if you see any sign of surveying.'

'Have you heard something?' she asked.

'No. Charlie Peascod is being unusually close-mouthed. Why don't you pop along this evening and see what's going on? Take your little girl with you. You can always say you're on a nature walk or something.'

'I'm not taking Ally with me! Suppose we're thrown out for trespassing?'

'We couldn't get that lucky.' Maybe her expression betrayed just how far he'd stepped over the line because he said, 'It's nearly lunchtime. You might as well go now. But don't take all day about it.'

The minute Bea had left, Hal walked across the courtyard towards the garages.

Claire's bike was standing, upended, still minus a wheel, in one corner. It had been more than a week since her bike had been damaged, too long for her to be without any kind of transport. And when it was fixed she wouldn't have an excuse to ring him.

'Gary?'

There was a clank of metal, the familiar sound of a spanner hitting concrete, followed by a muttered oath.

He followed the sound to the workshop and the

years rolled back as he saw the boy and an old motorcycle in pieces strewn all around him.

The minute Claire got home, she changed into jeans, boots and, with her camera tucked into her pocket, she walked down to the meadow.

It was a classic flower meadow. It hadn't been ploughed in centuries, just grazed by sheep, rabbits and Archie. Except that Archie wasn't there.

Forget looking for surveyors setting up levels, she had to talk to Hal, find out what on earth was going on.

'Okay, hand me the nut…'

'This one?'

Hal, lying on his side as he tackled an awkward connection, turned his head a little too quickly and nearly lost the assembly he was rebuilding.

Claire Thackeray, all legs in a pair of close-fitting jeans, was offering him a large wing nut.

'Don't be ridiculous,' he snapped. 'Anyone with half a brain cell can see that I need that one.'

'Pardon me.' She dropped the wing nut and bent to pick up the small nut he'd indicated, but instead of handing it to him, she closed her hand around it and straightened up. 'Where is Archie?' she asked.

Archie?

'The nut?' he prompted. It was taking a considerable amount of pressure to hold everything in place.

'He's not in his meadow.'

She was serious?

'I don't want another quad-bike incident.'

'I shouldn't have sent you that link,' she said, ignoring the irritable clicking of his fingers. 'What have you done with him, Hal?'

'Give me that nut and I'll tell you.' She offered it between finger and thumb. 'It may have escaped your notice,' he said, through gritted teeth, 'but I can't let go of this.'

She took a step closer, close enough for him to smell the crushed grass on her boots, see the way her jeans stretched across her hips, clung to a backside his hand remembered.

'Will you get down here?'

His voice felt as if it was wading through treacle.

She dropped to her knees and now he had the full impact of skin glowing from a brisk walk, wisps of cream-coloured hair escaping the clasp at her neck, huge grey eyes.

The wish-fairy come to life…

He closed his hand around the nut and discovered that her hand was shaking. Or was it his?

For a moment their gazes locked. It was his thumb, the one holding the spring assembly together, on the point of losing it, that reminded him what he was supposed to be doing. He took the nut, fastened it in place. 'Pass me a spanner.'

She glanced at the row of tools and, wonder of wonders, selected the right one.

'Now, hold this.'

'It's greasy,' she objected.

'Tough, it's you or Gary and I don't see Gary. What have you done with him?

'I made the magic sign of the teacup. I had to talk to you, Hal.'

'Nice try, Claire, but I don't...'

'No comment won't cut it. This isn't work.'

'It's not?' She really was worried about that stupid donkey? 'In that case we're both playing hooky. I'm recapturing my boyhood, what's your excuse?'

'The usual. Rumour, drivel...'

'Then it can wait until we've finished this.' And he kept her there for half an hour, handing him parts as he worked on the bike.

A smear of grease appeared on her cheek, on her shirt. She gritted her teeth as her hand slipped and she knocked a knuckle, but didn't complain. By the time they'd finished she was anticipating his next move and they were working smoothly as a team.

'Anyone would think you'd done this before,' he said, passing her a cloth to wipe her hands.

'I may have taken my lawnmower to bits once or twice.'

'You are full of surprises,' he said, standing up, offering his hand to help her to her feet. 'Shall we go and see if Gary managed to switch on the kettle?' He glanced back at her as they crossed the courtyard. 'I don't suppose you brought that cake you keep threatening me with? Or have you been too busy earthing up your potatoes?'

'Hal...'

'Archie's in the stables,' he said, taking pity on her. 'He's been confined to barracks until the hedging contractor has made the meadow escape-proof.'

'Oh.'

'Why? What did you think I'd done with him?'

'Nothing.' She said it too quickly. 'Just... One of my colleagues said something. Nothing.'

'Hardly nothing if it had you racing up here to check up on him.'

She pulled a face. 'Just a stupid throwaway remark.' He waited. 'It involved the phrase "cats' meat."'

He would have been affronted if she hadn't been so obviously embarrassed. If she hadn't been so desperately concerned.

'I suppose I should be grateful that you bothered to check rather just starting a hue and cry with a story about a missing donkey.'

'We're not so short of stories at the *Observer* that we're reduced to manufacturing them. I've been remarkably restrained.'

'Am I supposed to be grateful?'

'I haven't written a word about being attacked by livestock running wild on a public footpath, my trashed bicycle, the cuts and bruises I sustained without so much as a penny-piece in compensation from the landowner. On the contrary, it was the landowner who demanded—'

'Why not?' he asked, cutting short her list of complaints.

Claire looked at the cloth, rubbed at a stubborn grease spot, grateful for the interruption. If she reminded Hal about the on-the-spot fine he'd levied, he might also recall how enthusiastically she'd paid up.

'You know why not,' she said. 'He's had enough bad press.'

'That doesn't explain why you're going easy on me. Isn't it your public duty to warn your fellow citizens about my wicked past?'

He was closer. Too close…

'You haven't mentioned the poaching,' he pointed out. 'Or the graffiti on Cranbrook's factory walls, or the time I rode a motorcycle up the venerated steps of Cranbrook Hall and in through the front door. Why is that, Claire?'

'You were a kid. I'm more interested in what you're doing now.' Which was the truth. This was a different world, they were different people… 'Were you?' she asked. 'Wicked?'

His smile took her unawares and, as he caught her hand, the heat of it went straight to her knees, burning up her lips, firing the same melting ache between her thighs as his kiss…

'Do you want to come inside and repeat that question?' he offered.

'I'll take that as a yes,' she managed, her voice remarkably steady considering the fact that the rest of her appeared to be slowly melting.

'Good decision,' he said.

Was it? Right now melting was deeply appealing.

The thought of being touched by those oil-stained hands, being kissed, being wicked...

'Did you really ride your motorbike through the front door of Cranbrook Hall?' she asked.

'You hadn't heard about that?' He seemed surprised.

'No one ever talked to me.' Oh, good grief, that sounded so pathetic. 'Was that why Sir Robert banned you from the estate?'

'It wasn't Sir Robert who did that, Claire, it was your father.' And his hand slid from hers, leaving her feeling oddly bereft.

'My dad?'

'Acting on Robert Cranbrook's instructions I have no doubt, but he enjoyed delivering the message.'

'I didn't know.' She swallowed. 'Not that it matters,' she added quickly. 'I'm far more interested in how you progressed from estate tearaway to millionaire businessman.'

'Are you?' His doubt suggested, worryingly, that he knew exactly the effect he had on her. 'Well, you're the journalist, if a somewhat ineffectual one judging by your performance so far. You won't get far in your chosen profession unless you toughen up, learn to be ruthless.'

'Is that how you succeeded?'

'There is no other way. The difference between us is that in your business it doesn't matter who you hurt so long as you sell newspapers.'

She opened her mouth to protest. Closed it. Took a breath. 'I told you, this has nothing to do with my job.'

'A real journalist is never off duty, Claire.'

'Then I guess I'm not a real journalist...'

There was moment of shocked silence as the reality of what she'd just said sank in.

'So, what? You're just playing at it?'

She shook her head, as if to deny it but her mouth was clamped tight and Hal felt a moment of pity for her. What the hell was she doing in a job she clearly wasn't cut out for?

'Would it reassure you if I told you that I was the one who used apples to train Archie to be my wing man?' he said.

He saw the ripple in her neck as she swallowed hard, taking a mental step back from what she'd just said.

'Wing man?'

'Once he got the hang of being bribed to be quiet, he kicked up a fuss whenever anyone came near.'

'Giving you time to disappear.' A smile broke

through, lighting up her eyes. 'That would be the same apples,' she said. 'From the tree in my garden?'

'It would.'

She shook her head. 'Now I feel really stupid.'

'You look it. Here…' He took her chin in her hand, lifted her face and taking the cloth she was holding, wiped at the smear of grease.

Her skin was warm against his fingers and her soft pink lips, parted as if to ask a question she'd thought better of, invited a kiss. Not the harsh, punishing kiss he'd inflicted on her that day on the path, that she'd subverted into something else, but the kind that could only ever have one conclusion.

'Has it gone?' she asked.

'No, I've just made it worse,' he said, dropping his hand, turning away.

Not in this lifetime.

'You'd better come inside and clean up. You don't want to be on the street looking like that.' Gary was in the kitchen, emptying the biscuit tin. 'Lunch break's over,' he said. The lad looked startled and Hal being aware that he'd been abrupt said, 'We'll finish your bike tomorrow.'

'Really? Gosh, thanks, Mr North… Hal. Actually…' He waited. 'Would you mind if I

brought a mate with me to watch? We're hoping
to start a scramble team and—'

'Yes, yes,' he said. 'Now get back to work.'

'That's kind of you,' she said, when Gary had
gone.

'It's nothing. Pure self-indulgence.'

'Helping Gary isn't nothing. Recapturing your
boyhood isn't nothing.'

'I don't have time for that.'

'No?' She gave a little sigh. 'Growing up isn't all
it's cracked up to be, is it? I'd better go and wash
my hands.'

'I'll be in the morning room.'

Claire used the staff cloakroom to clean up, splashing cold water onto her face and neck to cool herself down.

Standing out there in the courtyard she'd been
sure that Hal was going to kiss her again and not
to punish her this time, even if she deserved it.

For one reckless, forget-the-world moment, she'd
wanted him to. She scooped up more water,
splashed herself again. Gathered the ends of
her hair and re-fastened the clip. Tidying everything up. Restoring order out of the chaos of her
thoughts, her life.

Blanking out that moment when he'd challenged her and the ground had seemed to open up in front of her. What on earth was she thinking?

Not a real journalist…

A glance in the mirror belied any hope of order.

She wasn't about to use anti-bacterial hand wash on her face and she'd been a bit too enthusiastic with the splashing. Her shirt was wet, almost transparent. She had to change, get back to work. Bad enough to be going back empty-handed, but late buses was an excuse that she could only take so far.

Hal wasn't in the kitchen and she pushed open the green baize door that divided upstairs from downstairs. She'd expected it to be stripped bare, but it was much as she remembered, family portraits and all.

'Having a good look round?'

'I'm just surprised it's all still here, but I don't suppose there's much of market for second-hand ancestors.'

'It depends whose ancestors they are,' he said.

She glanced at him.

'There's no one here important enough, distinguished enough to excite anyone who isn't a Cranbrook, and the previous owner's nursing-home room isn't big enough to accommodate them.'

'Poor man. It must be so difficult for him.'

'He made bad choices, Claire. He has to live with them.'

He sounded, looked so hard.

'Have you never made a bad choice?' she asked.

'I got married.' For a moment she thought he was going to say more, but he just looked at her. 'What about you?'

'I fell in love with the wrong man,' she said. 'I'm not sure that choice had much to do with it but I let down my family.'

'And Robert Cranbrook let down his.'

'I suppose.' She looked up at a portrait of Sir Robert's mother, holding her son. There was a faded border around it, where there had once hung a larger portrait of his father, replaced when it was damaged. 'So,' she said, turning away, looking around at the serried ranks of Cranbrooks rising up the stairs, 'the portraits were thrown in with the fixtures and fittings. Like unwanted carpets and curtains.'

'I can almost see the cogs turning in your brain. It's not a story, Claire.'

'Isn't it?' Something told her that it was, but she let it go. 'I told you, I'm off the clock.'

'So you did. Shall we take these into the morning room?'

He handed her a mug and led the way to a small, shabby but comfortable sitting room with French windows that stood open on to a sunken walled rose garden.

She carried her mug onto the terrace.

'It breaks my heart to see it in this state,' she said, sipping at her tea. 'It makes my fingers itch to get stuck in with the sécateurs.'

'You love gardening?'

'There's something about restoring order out of chaos that appeals to me,' she said. 'And then putting back just enough chaos to make it interesting.'

'You'll find all the chaos you need here. This has been neglected since Cranbrook's wife left him. Fortunately, it's not like the Hall, where every single item of architectural detail has to be approved before it can be replaced.'

'Replaced?' She looked up at him. 'Please tell me that you're not planning to grub it up? Plant tidy rows of bedding plants. All the same colour, the same height…'

'You said it. Order out of chaos.'

'I didn't mean… Some of these roses are really old, Hal. Heritage varieties.'

'Old, dying, heritage varieties.'

'It takes more than neglect to kill a rose. These just need some TLC. You should consult a specialist. You might be able to interest a grower in a restoration project.'

'And have sponsorship signs all over the place? I'll stick to the bedding plants, thanks.'

'All they'd want is a discrete little plaque somewhere, acknowledging their contribution. I've seen them in other great gardens.'

'So what do they get out of it?'

'In this case I imagine they'd love the chance to take cuttings, use modern methods to breed from your old varieties,' she offered. 'Their PR people would commission a book on the restoration project—you could sell it to your guests—and provide articles for gardening magazines, the Sunday supplements, lifestyle magazines. Everyone wins.' She put down the mug, aware that she was letting her passion run away with her tongue. 'I have to get back to work, Hal.'

'Next time bring cake.'

'Is that an open invitation? I do a great Victoria sandwich with homemade raspberry jam—'

'Goodbye, Claire.'

'I make the jam myself,' she said, her mouth running away with her, even while her head was saying, 'Go. Now.' 'With raspberries from my garden.'

'That would be perfect. And don't forget that you owe Archie two applies.'

'Two?' He'd remembered her desperate appeal as she was chased down the path? 'While I'd be the first to admit that Archie is a smart donkey, I doubt he keeps a tally,' she said. 'Besides, since he didn't deliver on the deal, I don't think he has a leg to stand on.'

'Then just come yourself. He gets lonely.'

'What about you, Hal? This is a big place to live in on your own.'

'Two apples, a Victoria sandwich,' he said, 'and you can send me the name of a rose specialist. Just in case I change my mind.'

CHAPTER SEVEN

HAL stood at the open French windows, listening to a blackbird sing, trying to blot out the image of Claire Thackeray.

Her concerns for an old donkey, a neglected garden, for Gary were beginning to eat away at his armour, undermine his determination to visit the sins of the father on her head.

Bea was right. He should have left this to the professionals.

Claire walked home, her head in a whirl, scarcely noticing where she put her feet. Talk about the good news and the bad news…

All she'd wanted to do was reassure herself that Archie was okay. Job done. But walking into the courtyard and seeing Hal on his back with a motorcycle in bits around him had been a heart-leap moment, a flashback to the boy in leathers astride his own bike. Today, though, she hadn't been an outsider. She'd been there, working alongside him and for a while had felt like a kid herself.

It couldn't last.

On some subconscious level, she'd always known that her father must have been involved in Hal's banishment. He'd been the estate manager, he ran Cranbrook Park. He engaged and dismissed staff, dealt with maintenance, arranged shoots and fishing parties.

Keeping order had been his responsibility.

She might be reduced to jelly-bones by Hal, but she could well understand why he'd been so peppery when they'd met. It hadn't just been the crash. She was a Thackeray and in his shoes she wouldn't have wanted to have anything to do with her, either.

She was amazed that he answered her phone calls. He could easily have left them to Penny, or let them go to voice mail. And he'd listened to her on the rose garden. That was good news. It would mean he was invested in Cranbrook Park, in the Hall.

As for that moment when he'd challenged her commitment to her job, being a journalist was what she did.

It put food on the table, kept Ally safe. It was

what she'd always been going to do. She might not be working for the BBC, or be a high-flying correspondent for one of the broadsheets, but she was doing her best to fulfil the ambitions of her parents. Speaking of which—

She sat on a grassy bank, took out her phone and called Brian.

'Where on earth have you been?' he demanded.

'It's a big estate, Brian, but I haven't seen any sign of surveying so far.'

'Nothing?'

'Nothing.' Which was true. 'But I have heard a whisper that Mr North is thinking about restoring the rose garden.'

'And?'

'It's a famous garden. Bags of history.' She glanced at her watch. 'It'll be a waste of time coming back to the office. I'll do some research at home and maybe we can run something tomorrow?'

'We're running the Teddy Bear's Picnic story tomorrow.'

'I haven't finished it.'

'I have. Mr Mean Targets Teddies. The garden story can go in the home supplement on Saturday.'

She muttered an expletive she wouldn't have used at home and dialled again.

'North.'

'Hal…'

'Claire… Twice in one day.'

'Sorry, but I need to talk you out of cancelling the Teddy Bears Picnic.'

'Sorry.'

'Not a chance?'

'No.'

'That's a shame. The news editor's wife is the treasurer of the animal-rescue charity that benefits from the event.'

'Then I'll brace myself for tomorrow's edition.'

'Don't buy it unless you want to see a really sweet photograph of you, aged six, dressed as one of the three bears in a primary-school play on the front page,' she said,

'I take back everything I said. You are ruthless.'

'Absolutely,' she said, heart sinking.

'Why don't they hold it at Memorial Park?' he suggested.

'You're not getting it. We need woods. If you go down to the woods today…?' She sang a snatch of the song.

'You are not doing your case any favours.'

'You've got until the paper goes to press to reconsider.'

'Don't hold your breath.'

'No. Right. Breathing in and out.' She didn't want to hang up. 'I forgot to ask Gary when my bike will be ready.'

'Apparently they don't make wheels like that any more but he's doing his best to find a second-hand replacement. I'd buy you a new bike, but I'm sure you'd just tell the world I'm trying to buy your silence.'

'Not the world,' she assured him, saying goodbye to any chance of that. 'Just Maybridge.'

'Shame. I saw one on the Net that would have been perfect. Pink and white. Just like the one you had when you were a little girl.'

'I'm all grown up now, Hal.'

'Goodbye, Claire.

Hal picked the newspaper out of the bin, looked again at the fairy lookalike. Claire's hair was still the colour of rich cream with a tendency to escape the tortoiseshell clip she used to hold it back and curl in soft tendrils around her face. It was the kind of clip that gave a man ideas. Which was, no doubt, its purpose.

Not that he needed any help.

At a distance, he could be rational about her. Remember that she was the daughter of his enemy.

Close up, with her scent—a combination of shampoo, soap, the memory of bluebells—blanking out the smell of motor oil, her eyes smiling even when her mouth was trying not to, her mouth smiling because she forgot to keep it in line, he'd wanted a re-run of a kiss that should never have happened. To feel her body soften in response to him the way it had that morning on the path.

Taking Claire Thackeray in a ditch… Against one of the estate's ancient oaks… In the Queen's bed…

All grown up and he knew that he'd dream about letting loose her lovely hair to fall over pale, naked shoulders.

Daydream when he should be concentrating on the ballroom ceiling.

Night dream about doing things with raspberry jam that would put it on the Women's Institute banned list but, more to the point, what was she going to do about him?

So far, she'd stuck strictly to the facts, although that first piece might have raised a wry smile amongst those who remembered him.

He'd anticipated some comeback to his crack about her not fulfilling her mother's inflated expectations. It had hurt her. It had been his intention to hurt her.

She had been the estate's little princess while he'd been the frog who was supposed to live under a stone.

So why hadn't she struck back hard? She knew that he'd been thrown off the estate and that was the story any real journalist would have told.

But then no real journalist would have warned him about what was going to be on tomorrow's front page.

He called up the *Observer*'s website and clicked on the link to the editorial staff. She was about halfway down the list, a cool blonde looking out at the world with a confident smile, very different from the mud-spattered creature, hair tumbled about her face that he'd picked out of the ditch. Full of sass and spirit one minute, flapping her eyelashes at him the next, when she thought he might be useful to her.

Still the estate princess despite her fall from grace. She might have been bright, but not bright enough to avoid the obvious trap.

Knowing her mother, he'd have thought an unwanted pregnancy would have involved a quick trip to the nearest clinic. But maybe it hadn't been an unwanted pregnancy. After all, she'd told him herself, she'd been in love.

Not wanting to think about it, he swept the paper up, but as he was about to drop it where it belonged, in the waste-basket, his attention was caught once again by the fairy perched on the masthead.

He was here to make her pay, but so far she'd been doing all the running. It was time to bite back.

'Okay, everyone. Can I have your attention for a moment?' Jessica Dixon, the assistant editor, stood in the centre of the large open-plan newsroom and looked around. 'As you all know we launched this year's "Make a Wish" campaign last week and we've had lots of interesting suggestions.' She glanced at the card she was holding. 'A facelift for the Guildhall—'

'That'll be the mayor trying to get it done on the cheap.'

'If it keeps the Council Tax down I'm all for that.'

'The Mums & Minis group are pushing for an undercover children's play area in Memorial Park and we've had several requests to restore the riverside gardens after last year's bad weather,' she continued determinedly, ignoring several more sarcastic remarks. 'There have also been a lot of great ideas to help individual people in need. It will be our Fairy Godmother's job to liaise with local youth groups and—' she looked around '—the really good news is that this year we have a sponsor for the Make a Wish scheme.'

'A sponsor? Does that mean our fairy will have to wear a company logo on her wings?' someone joked.

'No logo. Our sponsor isn't a company, but a private individual and we have Claire to thank for that.'

Claire, busy on a piece of village-school closures, looked up when she heard her name.

'What?' she asked. 'What have I done?'

'Quite a lot, apparently,' Tim said, with what could only be described as a snigger. 'It seems that your one-woman campaign to rouse the community spirit of a new arrival in the area has borne fruit.'

It took her a moment to filter through the background sound. The guildhall...sponsorship...her campaign...new arrival...

Hal?

'Are you saying that this year's Make a Wish is going to be sponsored by Henry North?'

'By George, I think she's got it!'

Hal was getting involved with the Make a Wish scheme? Why did that make her nervous?

'What exactly is he offering? His money, his time or his labour?' she asked, trying not to think about the powerful muscles beneath that green coverall, the soft cashmere. 'And, more to the point, what does he want in return?'

Jessica sketched the smallest of shrugs. 'All I know is that in return for supporting whatever major "Wish" we decide to undertake this year, Mr North has asked for just two things. One, that we help him with a Wish of his own—'

'A Wish? The man's a multimillionaire, what can we do for him?' someone asked.

'Give Claire the sack?' Tim suggested, dodging as she threw the latest edition of the paper at him. She missed him but clean-bowled his coffee cup, splattering him with cold dregs. A result.

Life was tough enough without him suggesting that she was surplus to requirements.

'And two,' Jessica continued, 'since he'll be

working with her, he's asked to be allowed to choose this year's Fairy Godmother.'

'I bet it'll be some model he's dating...'

'Yes, please! That would guarantee us a mention in *Celebrity* magazine...'

'No!' Then as everyone turned to stare, Claire said, 'He doesn't do that kind of publicity.'

'Oh? And how would you know?'

'She's the local authority on Henry North,' Tim said again.

'Actually, it can't be an outsider,' she said quickly as she once again became the centre of attention. 'It has to be someone on the staff...'

Nooooooo... But even as the words left her lips she knew what was coming and instinctively slumped down in her chair, ducking behind her monitor.

'Quite right, Claire,' Jessica said, approvingly. 'This isn't a media circus, it's about community so if you could spare a moment? Mrs Armstrong would like a word.'

Tim, mopping up the sunrise splatter of cold coffee dregs from his shirt, paused long enough to shout an ironic, 'Goal!'

'Claire's been called out of the office,' she said,

from behind her computer. If she was going to be the office joke, she was entitled to the laughs.

'Chasing down yet another investigative piece for the front page?'

Her trip to London on expenses had not gone unnoticed, or uncommented on.

'Only if she's investigating the dust under her desk.'

A ripple of laughter ran around the office and, straightening up, Claire held up a dust-coated finger. 'Actually, it's a vital and wide-ranging report on Health and Safety in the workplace.'

'Shouldn't that be "elf and safety"?'

'Who needs a duster when you've got a magic wand?'

'Everyone's a comedian,' she said, pushing her seat back and doing her best to put a brave face on things. 'If Mr North has seen the error of his ways and is prepared to salve his conscience by helping with a project that benefits the town, let's make it a good one. Something to make his eyes water.'

Toughen up, be ruthless...

Meanwhile, in return for sprinkling the fairy dust of publicity on local suppliers who supported the "Wish"—free promo in the paper in return for their generosity—and hours of extra unpaid work spent drumming up that support, chasing down grants, organising local youth groups, she was about to be working with Hal North. Given the choice, she wouldn't have done it dressed in a tutu and wings.

She paused just before she reached the door and, having pasted on a broad grin for her colleagues, she turned to face them and was confronted by the display of the week's front pages.

Mr Mean Targets Teddies leapt out at her.

Oh, well, brave face, Claire...

'Ladies, gentlemen...' She waved her ballpoint over them with a flourish before executing a low curtsey. 'I leave you to fight over the front page while I don my wings and fly away to part Mr Mean from his money.'

She'd anticipated an ironic cheer. At the very least a laugh. What she got was dead silence. She flicked a glance in Tim's direction. He was always good for a jeer, if nothing else. He'd paused in the act of mopping the coffee off his shirt but didn't respond with as much as a twitch of an eyebrow and with a sudden sick feeling in the pit of her stomach she turned around.

Behind her, Willow Armstrong, the CEO of the Melchester-based Armstrong Newspaper Group which owned not only the *Maybridge Observer,* the *County Chronicle* and dozens of other titles in the region, but the local commercial radio station, was standing in the corridor.

With her, Hal North, a head taller, was looking down his long, not-quite-straight nose; piercing her with eyes that were of a blue so intense, so dark that it sucked the breath right out of her body.

'Hal…' Willow Armstrong, ignoring the pregnant silence said, 'I believe you know Claire Thackeray?'

'We have met,' he said. His expression was grave, serious, but a gleam in the depths of those eyes suggested that he was enjoying the moment even if she was not.

No green coveralls today, not a trace of motor oil, but a lightweight grey tweed suit that was exactly right for the well-heeled gentleman about his business in a country town.

'Claire, Mr North has read about our "Make A Wish for Maybridge" programme and has generously offered to support us this year. Since you've shown such a passionate interest in Cranbrook Park,' she added smoothly, not suggesting by as much as a flicker of an eyelash that she'd seen that

'Mr Mean' headline, 'he has asked to work with you on the flagship project.'

This was her prompt to say something, but clearly not the word that had momentarily threatened to slip from her lips. Fortunately, with his gaze holding her like a moth on a pin and the breathless silence of the editorial office behind her, words—as ridiculous as that seemed—had deserted her.

This was her big chance to get close to him, she told herself. Not in a ditch or over a motorcycle, but a chance to talk to him, find out where he'd been, what he'd been doing all these years.

Why he'd come back.

She could write an in-depth profile of a very successful, very private businessman. Something that mattered. Something bigger than the *Observer* could handle, but would make a colour spread in the *County Chronicle,* the group's glossy lifestyle magazine. Maybe even make a national newspaper. Something that would lift her career a notch or two.

She should be happy…

Jessica's surreptitious nudge in the back was sufficient to make her blink and the break in eye contact restored a little of her composure. She breathed in, placed her hand in his.

'Hal…' she said. 'How unexpected. You're always telling me that you never talk to the press.'

'Is that why you haven't called recently?'

'There seemed no point.'

'Never give up, Claire. Given sufficient incentive—' his hand closed around hers in what was less a conventional handshake, more a 'gotcha' moment as he held it a little too firmly for her to pull away without making it obvious '—I'm prepared to talk to anyone.'

'It was the Victoria sandwich that did it?'

'I expected you to bring it yourself.'

'I've been a bit busy.' She swallowed. 'What kind of support are you offering the Make a Wish project?' she asked, doing her best to ignore the continuing firm pressure of his cool fingers around her own.

Cold hand, warm heart?

Her own fluttered a little as she recalled the way her cold lips had heated up as he'd kissed her, his long fingers encircling her ankle, sliding between her toes. That moment when he wiped the oil from her cheek.

Her knees buckled.

Her lips burned…

She rested her free hand on the door handle, told

herself to get a grip. So, Brian had stuck a vile headline on a story with her name on it. It was Hal who'd told her that it didn't matter who you hurt as long as you sold newspapers.

'You're in the transport business, aren't you?' she managed, as if her file on him didn't contain the exact number of vehicles his company operated, the total tonnage of air cargo, shipping containers it had handled in the last tax year. When his transport company was floated on the stock exchange a couple of years back his business—if not his life—had become public property. 'We always need help moving the goods people donate.'

'I was thinking of something a little more hands on than that,' he replied.

There was the slightest tightening of his grip before he released her without warning, leaving her feeling weirdly off balance, as if she had been the one hanging on. Without his support the ground seemed to slip from beneath her feet and she found herself clinging to the door handle to stop herself slithering down it to the floor. Before she could take a step back, grab a breath, steady herself, his hand had shifted to her elbow. It should have helped.

No...

'Let's discuss it over a cup of coffee.'

'Coffee?' she repeated stupidly, her pulse quickening even as she clung to the door handle as if to a lifeline.

She was keen as mustard to discuss all and everything with him over coffee or any other beverage he had in mind—if he was going to make her pay for that headline, it was going to be a two-way street—but he was up to something. She needed to marshal her thoughts, marshal her knees, marshal everything before she could handle this.

Her boss, her editor were watching. It was vital to be professional.

Cool…

Who was she kidding? His hand was warming her skin through her sleeve, a flush of heat that was spreading up her arm, through her body, touching her with an intimacy that was disturbing, unnerving, arousing…

'Sadly, that won't be possible,' she said, hoping that she didn't sound as desperate as she felt. Breathe, breathe… 'Coffee will have to wait for another day,' she said, with every appearance of regret. 'I'm sure Willow has explained that Fairy Godmother duties are voluntary? My job has first priority and I'm interviewing a local woman who gave birth to triplets—' a story that had filled to-day's front page thank goodness '—in twenty min-utes. It's one of those human-interest stories our readers love and, since I'll be walking to the ma-ternity unit, I need to leave now,' she added.

After that, she was taking an early lunch so that she could take Ally home. It was half term this week and since Penny was now working five mornings a week for Hal, and Ally and Savannah had fallen out, childcare had become a lot more complicated.

Having demonstrated her independence, she managed a smile.

'Perhaps Ms Webb could give me a call and ar-range a convenient time for a meeting?' she sug-gested. 'I'd be happy to come up to the Hall. I know how busy you must be. How's the motorcy-cle coming along?'

A small crease deepened at the side of his mouth, his eyes darkened imperceptibly, acknowledging the tiny prod about her bicycle, about not talking to the press, but it had been a mistake to mention the motorcycle.

'And the rose garden?'

Shut. Up.

'Why don't I give you a lift to the maternity unit

and you can advise me on bedding plants over lunch?' he suggested. 'You do eat lunch?'

'Oh…' The sound escaped before she could stop it, betraying her annoyance that he refused to play by anyone's rules but his own.

She hated losing control. She'd done it once but had created order out of the chaos of her life, making a home, creating a garden, bringing up her little girl…

Belay that.

She'd lost control when she'd run into him on that footpath. Bad enough, but with nobody's job safe, having to rely on public transport to get anywhere and her childcare arrangements in ruins, she was juggling eels while running uphill.

'Don't worry about the triplets.' Willow stepped in before she could say something she regretted. 'I've been dying for an excuse to see them and I think I can still write a paragraph or two that won't shame the *Observer.*'

'Oh, but…'

'Jessica was telling me that you've got childcare issues?' Her smile was sympathetic. 'School holidays are a nightmare. Believe me, I know.'

Terrific! Thank you, Jessica.

'Actually, I've been talking to Brian,' she continued, 'and we're agreed that now the Make a Wish scheme has grown so large it needs someone whose sole responsibility is to co-ordinate it. Liaise with local companies, the voluntary and youth groups, keep an overview of progress, that sort of thing.'

'Yes?' *No!*

'He's offered to release you from his team for the next couple of months.'

Months!

'But…'

…I'm a journalist.

The words stuck in her throat as she realised exactly what Hal had done.

'You can handle the Wishes from home just as easily as the office, which will make life a little easier for you and,' she added, 'you will make a delightful Fairy Godmother.'

'Are you sure?' she said, making one last bid for her job. 'If it's authenticity you're after, maybe I could point you in the direction of Jessica?' If she was going down, she was going down fighting. 'She looks exactly like the grandmotherly FGM in Ally's book of fairy tales.'

Willow laughed, patted her arm as if she appreciated the joke, but then said, 'Hal has some really interesting ideas that you'll want to include in the voting list on Saturday, so I suggest you start there. Send me a weekly update and anything you need just ask.' She didn't wait for an answer but turned to Hal. 'I'll tell Mike that you're looking for local craftsmen, Hal. I'm sure he'll know someone who can help with your ceiling.'

'Thank you, Willow. I appreciate that.'

She glanced at her watch. 'The triplets!'

They both watched in silence as, having tossed her metaphorical hand grenade, she moved quickly to the front door to avoid the fallout.

'Impressive woman,' Hal said, finally.

'Yes. She is.' Her idol as it happened. They'd gone to the same school, although she'd been years later and Willow Armstrong had started as a journalist on their sister paper in Melchester, doing the 'human interest' stories, just like her. That was as far as the comparison went. Willow had been offered a job on a national newspaper but had turned it down, choosing instead to stay in Melchester and manage the Armstrong group. 'And a busy one,' she added. 'She's not just a figurehead, she really does run the whole show.'

'That would explain why you appeared to be so

shocked that she would drop everything to meet me here this morning.'

'Not at all.' That wasn't what had shocked her and they both knew it. 'Let's face it, you're not some nobody to be fobbed off on a local reporter. You're...'

'Mr Mean?' he offered when she hesitated.

She'd hesitated because she'd been going to say 'the lord of the manor' but Sir Robert had always had time for her. Unlike Hal North, who had mocked her lack of ambition and then used his power to take her away from the news desk. Sideline her.

Taking her silence for agreement, he said, 'You're a local reporter, aren't you?'

'Not much of one according to you.'

'You've sharpened up your act since then.'

'I took your advice, Hal. Nothing personal.'

'I think Mr Mean is about as personal as it gets, Claire. The fact that you haven't been back to see Archie, asked Gary to deliver your cake, suggests you're aware of that.'

'I told you, I've been busy. There's so much to do in the garden at this time of year.'

'I know. The contractor is going to be clearing the rose garden next week.'

'Hal!'

He said nothing.

'Didn't you contact any of the rose specialists I sent you?'

'I've been busy. I have a company to run, as well as a house to restore.'

'And motorcycles to play with.'

'That, too.'

'I'll do it for you—'

'Not unless you can wave your magic wand. You're going to be far too busy granting other people's wishes to work on your own.'

Working with Hal North Rule Number One: Keep it businesslike.

'We'd better get on with it, then. I'll see if the conference room is free. How do you take your coffee?'

'Not from a machine,' he replied. The hand at her elbow tightened imperceptibly as he began to steer her firmly in the direction of the door.

The heat increased a degree, tingling dangerously.

Claire told herself that it was anger rather than attraction. The sizzle that seemed to fry the air whenever they were in the same room was real enough, but he wasn't interested in her. Nor, she suspected, was he interested in the Wish project.

Whatever fairy tale he'd told Willow Armstrong his return to Cranbrook Park was tied up with what Sir Robert had done to him. What her father had done to him.

He'd dealt with Sir Robert, but her father wasn't alive to answer for his actions. Apparently she was going to have to stand in for him.

Working with Hal North Rule Number Two: Keep it totally businesslike.

She pointedly removed her elbow from his hand. 'I'll call your office and arrange a formal meeting at the Hall.'

She didn't wait for his agreement but walked back to her desk and began tossing all her belongings into her bag.

'Well, well, well,' Tim said to nobody in particular, 'that was a turn up for the book. The ambitious Miss Thackeray reduced to a playing Tinkerbell.'

'Book? What book?' she asked, refusing to rise to the bait. 'I didn't realise you had ever read a book, at least not one without pictures.'

'Sweet. Does Henry North have any idea what he's getting himself in for? The man must be a glutton for punishment.'

'Have a care, Tim, or I'll wave my wand and turn you into a frog.' She turned to look at him, then put her hand to her mouth. 'Oh, noooo… Someone's already done that.'

She gave him a little wave, put her bag over her shoulder and went through to collect Alice who was safely tucked up in the library working on a project under the eye of one of the juniors who was on filing duty.

'Come on, sweetheart.' She'd held off Hal North for the moment, but he wouldn't stay held off for long.

CHAPTER EIGHT

'NOT rushing off on my account, I hope.'

'Oh, sugar!' The betraying words slipped out as Hal North straightened from the wall he'd been leaning against, out of sight until she was through the front door.

'That was heartfelt. Why do I get the feeling that if you'd realised I was waiting you'd have left by the rear entrance?'

'Why on earth would I sneak out the back way?' Claire demanded, all the more indignant because it was true.

'I don't know. The words "rabbit" and "head-lights" came to mind when you saw me in your space for a change.'

'You're the one who avoids the press.'

'Oh, it was merely surprise? I thought perhaps you were worried that having poked your stick into my wasp's nest—'

'Don't worry, Hal, I get it,' she said. 'I've been stung.'

He hadn't complained about her, hadn't got her the sack. Instead, he'd got her taken off the news desk, placed at his beck and call for weeks on end and had himself officially transformed from Mr Mean into Mr Generous at a stroke.

There would be no more snarky headlines written by her, or anyone else.

A result in anyone's language.

'So, coffee,' she said briskly. 'Shall we try the café in the craft centre? It's Ally's favourite.'

'Ally?'

Ally, fed up with being taken to one boring place after another, having to be quiet and well-behaved instead of having fun like everyone else at half term, had been dragging her heels behind her, sliding down the wall with a sigh when she'd seen her mom stop to talk to someone. Not complaining, but thoroughly fed up.

Well, that was all about to change.

'Come and say hello to Mr North, sweetheart, he's going to buy you a milkshake.'

'A milkshake?' She scrambled to her feet, looked up at Hal. 'Seriously?'

'Seriously. You deserve one.' She picked up Hal's long, thoughtful look, smiled. 'I did give you every chance.'

'No. That would have meant you'd told me that you had your little girl with you,' he said in the same pleasant tone, his own smile pitch perfect. Then, before she could let him off the hook, tell him that she was going to drop her off at Penny's for the afternoon he turned to Ally and said, 'Tell me, Alice, is your heart set on a milkshake at the craft centre? Or could I possibly tempt you to lunch by the river?'

'Penny's making you lunch,' Claire said before she could answer. 'Spaghetti with meatballs. Your favourite,' she added, to soften the blow.

'But what about the milkshake?' she asked, with a confused little frown. Ally did a very good confused little frown.

'I'll make you one when I get home.'

'It's not the same,' she said. 'You can't make it so thick that you can hardly suck it through the straw.'

'Penny? Would that be Penny Harker?' Hal asked, rescuing her before she was promising double, triple scoops of strawberry ice cream in the shake. 'Gary's mother?'

'Yes. Of course you know her.'

'I know why she couldn't work this afternoon,' he said. 'Why she won't work full-time.'

'You asked her to work full-time?' Claire was shocked. 'I had no idea.'

'Well you do now so the least you can do is call and tell her you won't need her to babysit this afternoon. Make everyone's day.'

His day, Penny's day, Ally's day. She wasn't so sure about hers...

Leaving her to it, he turned to Ally and with the utmost seriousness said, 'Tell me, Alice, is the Birdcage still the best place in town for lunch?'

Ally's eyes widened. 'The Birdcage? Is that the place that looks like a birdcage? That has birds? In cages.'

'That sounds like the place.'

'I'm not sure I approve of birds in cages,' she said. 'Can they fly about? Not just hop around like Savannah's budgie?'

'Why don't you ask your mother? She used to go there all the time when she was your age.'

'I went there once!' Claire said, with a glare that warned him that making plans for her was one thing, making them with her daughter was quite another. 'And there is still a problem.'

'Why am I not surprised?' There was nothing in his voice, his manner to betray him and yet she sensed his impatience. He had a plan and she was messing with it. Tough. 'If you're worried about timekeeping I'll swear it was a working lunch.'

'What else would it be?' she snapped. Dammit, lunch with Hal should have been... Nothing. 'Unfortunately, and I'm really sorry about this—' it wouldn't hurt to apologise, no matter how insincerely '—but I imagine you were planning on going by car?'

'I wasn't going to walk,' he said, using the fob he was holding to unlock the doors of a glossy black Range Rover parked at the kerb.

'Well, that's it, you see. Ally doesn't have her booster seat with her and, as I'm sure you know, it's against the law for a child to travel in a car without one.' She waited for the count of three. 'I suppose, if your heart really is set on The Birdcage, we could catch the bus?'

'The bus?' Hal appeared to consider it. 'That's a possibility,' he said. 'Or Alice could use the booster seat that Bea had fitted for her little girl.'

He lifted an eyebrow, inviting her to counter his check.

Claire had none to offer. Her only thought was that the plum-voiced Ms Webb had a daughter who visited often enough for Hal to need a booster seat in his car.

No more than her journalistic antenna twitching. His relationships were news. There was no other reason for her to be interested. At all.

'Well…' she said. 'How great is that, Ally? I wasn't much older than you the one time I went to the Birdcage.' Emphasis on the 'one.'

'My mistake,' Hal said, as he lifted Ally up. She scrambled across onto the booster seat and quickly fastened her seat belt before any more objections were raised. 'Your mother talked about it so much that I assumed it must be a regular event. According to my mother,' he stressed, presumably to establish that he was not in the habit of gossiping with her mother. As if. 'Didn't you have a good time?'

She concentrated on checking Ally's seat belt then shut the door before turning to face Hal. 'Truthfully?'

'What else?' he asked.

'I hated every minute of it.'

'Really? Well, you weren't with me on that occasion,' he said as he opened the passenger door for her.

'My mother would never have invited you out to tea with a bunch of little girls.'

'With or without,' he agreed, with a wry smile.

'I was definitely not her type, a sentiment I returned with interest. But little girls would have been safe enough.'

'I don't doubt it. You had bigger fish to fry.'

She caught his eye and despite doing her best to be cool, she discovered that what she wanted to do most of all was smile right back at him.

Despite the bad start, the prospect of lunch with Hal North at a pretty riverside restaurant had a ridiculously uplifting effect on her. Which was, well, ridiculous.

'Let's see,' she said, doing her best to keep her feet firmly planted on the ground. She had to remember that he hated her father, was messing with her career and she knew practically nothing about his life since he'd left Cranbrook Park. Who knew what ulterior motive was driving him? 'It was my eighth birthday so you must have been about fourteen or fifteen...' She pretended to think about it, but she could remember exactly what he'd been doing—or at least who he'd been doing it with— the year she was eight.

She'd seen him from the back of her mother's car that day. She'd been dressed up for her tea party in a pink frilly nightmare of a dress and as they'd driven through the village she'd seen him standing at the bus stop with his arm around a girl in a skirt so short that her legs had looked ten yards long.

Her mother had kept her eyes on the road, but there had been a distinct 'tut' as they'd passed.

She, on the other hand, had been green with envy, turning round in her seat to stare until her mother had spotted her in the mirror and told her to sit up straight before she creased her dress.

'That,' she said, 'if I'm not mistaken, was the year you were going out with the incredibly, um, precocious Lily Parker.'

'Was it?' His eyes creased into a smile that warned her she'd said too much, remembered too well, betrayed an interest she would have denied with her last breath. 'Possibly, although I can't imagine that even Lily, with her undoubtedly precocious assets, lasted an entire year.'

'So many girls, so little time,' she said, as he held the door and then as she hesitated at the high step up, placed his hand on her bottom and boosted her up into the front seat. For a moment their eyes locked. It was like descending on a roller coaster. That sensation of falling, leaving your stomach behind...

Working with Hal North Rule Number Three: Don't make eye contact.

'I was desperately envious of her red-leather skirt,' she said, just so that he'd know that it was Lily she'd noticed, rather than him. 'I always swore I'd have one exactly like it when I was fourteen.'

'And did you?'

'Oh, please! Do you think my mother would have allowed me out of the house wearing something like that?'

'A clever girl like you would have found a way. Did you never climb out of your bedroom window?'

'Is that what Lily did?'

'That would be telling.'

In other words, yes, but by the time she was old enough there had been no one to be bad with. Make that no one she'd wanted to be bad with.

She shook her head. 'I had too much homework to spend my nights hanging around in Maybridge,' she said, turning away to pull down her seat belt. 'Okay, sweetheart?' she asked, twisting in her seat to smile at Ally as he shut the door and walked around to take the seat beside her.

Ally nodded but she was sitting very still, clearly anxious not to do anything to make this unexpected treat go away. She was really missing Savannah, but refused to talk about it.

'Okay?' he asked, when she'd called Penny.

'Fine.'

Not fine. He'd offered Penny a full-time job and she'd turned it down because she needed someone to look after Ally. She paid her, but not as much as Hal, who had apparently put all the estate staff on the same pay scale, and with the same benefits, as his HALGO staff. She couldn't match that kind of hourly rate.

'I'll talk to her about working full-time when I see her,' she said. 'So, what's wrong with your ceilings?'

'My ceilings?' He shrugged. 'A combination of old age,' he said, looking over his shoulder to check the traffic before pulling out, 'and a leaking roof.'

'Ouch. That sounds expensive.'

'It will be. You might be better occupied devoting your front page to the scourge of thieves who are stripping lead from the roofs of churches and listed buildings.'

'If you'd talked to me about it, I would have done.' She lifted her hand to her mouth. 'Oh, no. That's not possible. You don't talk to the press.'

'I'm talking to you.'

'Too late. I'm off the news desk.' She shrugged. 'Actually, with several million to spend on property I think I'd have chosen something rather less of a liability than Cranbrook Park.'

'Would you? And here was me thinking that you were in love with the place. All those Christmas parties in the great hall, picnics, gymkhanas courtesy of Sir Robert.'

'You can mock, but it's been the backdrop to my life since I was four years old,' she told him. 'It's a big part of local history and every stone is full of stories. That doesn't mean I'd want to be responsible for it. Or live in it.'

'I was born in Cranbrook,' he reminded her, 'which gives me a good few years on you, but you're in excellent company. My accountant would endorse the former sentiment and my PA would definitely agree with the latter.'

'Miss Webb doesn't enjoy country life? Or is that Mrs Webb?' she asked.

'Does it matter?'

'Not to me. Presumably it does to her.'

'She's Mrs Webb. Divorced but—'

'There's a lot of it about,' she said, not wanting to know about her 'buts.'

'Her problem isn't with country life, it's to do with country plumbing.'

'Wimp,' she murmured.

'I wouldn't let her catch you saying that,' he replied. There was nothing wrong with his hearing. Nothing wrong with any bit of him…

She was the problem. She had the wrong name.

She glanced back at Ally, but she was too busy looking out of the window to be interested in them.

'So?' She kept her voice light as she asked the big question. 'Why did you buy Cranbrook Park?'

They were paused at the traffic lights and he looked at her. 'Because I could?' he offered.

And then he smiled.

It was nothing spectacular as smiles went, no more than the tiniest contraction of lines fanning out from indigo eyes but the effect was like sticking wet fingers into a live socket and the fizz went all the way down to her toes.

'It's about power, then,' Claire said, doing her best to ignore the tingle. Was there anything more galling than getting that kind of a sexual buzz from a man you didn't want to fancy? That it would be crazy to fancy?

Working with Hal North Rule Number Four: Don't say anything that will make him smile.

'No, it's about a promise I made the day I left Cranbrook,' he replied. Clearly the memory was not a good one because he abruptly lost the smile and the tingle was reduced to something more like the aftermath of pins and needles.

It wasn't over, but you could breathe again.

'Really?' she said, working to keep it that way. 'Did you swear to return rich as Croesus and buy out the wicked baron?'

Bad mistake. As an anti-smile strategy it worked for him but she found her own imagination running wild with the mental picture of some over-the-top confrontation between Hal and Sir Robert as he parked his motorcycle on the marble floor of the entrance hall. The miscreant—in black leathers rather than armour—swearing a fierce oath to return and claim his rightful place. A modern version of the dispossessed knight.

No.

Really.

Why on earth would he do that? Besides, he'd already told her it wasn't that incident which had got him banned from the estate.

On the other hand he hadn't bothered to deny it. And why else would he ride in through the front door, if not to make some statement of intent.

'It's a bit of a cliché isn't it?' she suggested, pushing him to tell her what had really happened.

'Clichés are what happen in moments of high drama, Claire.'

True her own small drama had contained just about every cliché in the book, but it was his story she was interested in.

'What drama?' she asked. 'How high?'

More importantly, who had he made that promise to? His mother? Sir Robert? Or just himself? Who was still around who might know?

Her mother almost certainly, but they'd have to be on speaking terms before she could ask her.

His mother…

'How is your mother?' she asked.

He glanced at her, a slight frown buckling his forehead as, unsurprisingly he hadn't followed her thought processes. 'She's well enough. She's living in Spain.'

'Will we see her? What does she think of you buying the estate?'

'She doesn't know.'

'Oh.' Weirder and weirder… 'She was always very kind to me. I missed her when she left.' She looked at him, but his expression gave nothing away. 'After your father died.'

His mouth tightened. 'It was an accident waiting to happen. The towpath on a foggy night is no place for a drunk.'

'Hal…' she warned, with a touch to his arm, reminding him that they weren't alone. Curling her fingers back when he looked across at her. 'I'm sorry. I didn't know. About your dad.'

'Why would you? You were never around when he came home after closing time.'

'No.' Had he been a violent drunk, or a sullen one? She restrained a shiver. 'Even so it was a shocking thing.'

'Why don't you say what's really on your mind, Claire? Where was I when my mother needed me?'

'No… At least I assumed the ban was still in place,' she said. 'I begged my mother to speak to Sir Robert. It seemed so cruel.'

'Did you?' Was that a smile? Stupid question, her heart rate had gone through the roof… 'And did she?'

She shook her head. 'She said I didn't understand. That it wasn't that simple. That you'd never come back.'

'How wrong can you be?' He took the slip road off the ring road. 'Have you told her?'

'That you've bought Cranbrook Park? No.'

'Mothers. Always the last to know anything…'

He shrugged. 'Well, when you do you can inform her that she was wrong on both accounts. It wasn't the ban that kept me away.'

He slowed for the roundabout, his hand brushing her leg as he changed down. She jumped as his touch shot through her like a charge of electricity but he didn't appear to notice.

'The boring truth is that I was in India on business when it happened and my mother made sure that I didn't hear about it until it was all over and done with. I had her out of here the minute I did.' He glanced at her. 'She wouldn't leave before. In case you were wondering.'

'Why would I wonder? I had no idea you were so successful. Or that she might be unhappy.' She swallowed. 'I'm sorry, Hal.'

'Don't be. At least not for me.' He picked up speed, reached for the stick shift to change up but before she could move her knees out of the danger zone, he said, 'Jack North wasn't my natural father.'

Claire, stunned, opened her mouth, but couldn't think of a thing to say and closed it again.

Hal, shockingly, laughed. 'Could that be you losing the power of speech?' he asked.

'No!'

Not his father?

Well, that made sense in a weird sort of way. They hadn't been a bit alike...

'Well, maybe. Just a bit,' she admitted, with a rueful smile.

So who was? Someone on the estate? Who did he look like? There was something flickering in the back of her mind. Something she'd heard, maybe, or seen...

'Was that your intention?' she asked, refusing to ask him outright. If she'd learned anything in her brief dealings with Hal North, it was that if he wanted her to know something he'd tell her. If he didn't, he'd change the subject.

Then, suspiciously, 'Was it even true?'

Working with Hal North Rule Number Five: Don't believe everything he says.

'If it was my intention, clearly I'm going to have to try harder,' he said, turning off the road and pulling into the riverside car park. 'But why would I lie?'

'To wind me up?'

'Why would I bother when you do such a great job all by yourself.'

Okaaay...

Working with Hal North Rule Number Six: Disregard Rule Number Five.

But why would he tell her something so personal? Did he really believe that removing her from the news desk would totally silence her? Surely no man so careful of privacy would be that naive?

No way. He'd told her because it didn't matter. She'd mentioned the tragic accident in that first piece she'd written about him, but Jack North was a drunken labourer who'd fallen into the river and drowned one misty night. How much worse could it get?

No. He simply wanted to shock her. Send her off on some wild goose chase, no doubt. But while her curiosity was aroused she felt nothing but relief that she wouldn't have to write it.

Get this Wish thing over with and she'd happily report town-council meetings and agricultural shows until the cows came home.

He'd climbed out, opened Ally's door while she struggled to make sense of it. 'First one to the island gets an ice cream,' he said, as he lifted her down, then having wound her up, stood back to let her race away over the bridge.

'Oh, for goodness sake.' She scrambled down. 'Not before lunch!'

'And the milkshake you promised her?'

She glared at him. 'Don't go too close to the water, Ally!'

'Spoil sport.'

'Try responsible…' She sighed. 'Oh, never mind.'

He was right. She'd been happy enough to use a treat to wind up Hal and Ally was having a miserable half term. An ice cream would do no harm.

She walked on, Hal's hand still on her arm, holding her at his side as if fearing that she, too, might bolt, run on ahead.

'I'm sorry, Hal. It's half term. Jessie Michaels usually has her in the mornings. She and Savannah are best friends, were best friends. They've fallen out.'

'How are you managing?'

'Like every other woman in my situation. And every man. With a combination of help from my friends, expensive childcare and, when all else fails, doing what I did today and taking her with me to the office.'

'Not ideal.'

'No. She's being good, but it's a bit like living with a volcano with the lid on. You know it's going to blow and that the longer it takes the worse it's going to be.' She sighed. 'At least now, thanks to you, I can work at home.'

'You don't sound particularly grateful.'

'Forgive me if I don't weep with gratitude, Hal, but I don't think you meant to be kind.'

They'd reached the far end of the bridge where Ally was waiting for them, jumping up and down with excitement.

'I won, I won…'

'You beat us,' Hal said, taking a handful of coins from his pocket. 'Okay, let me see… I think I'll have a ninety-nine…' He looked at her. 'Claire?'

She shook her head but said, 'The same. A small one.'

'Two ninety-nines and whatever you want for yourself,' he said, dropping the change into Ally's upturned hands.

'She'll buy something ghastly with a load of E numbers,' Claire protested.

'Fuelling the volcano,' he said, taking her arm and heading along the bank. 'We'll be looking at the ducklings, Alice,' he called back.

'This is ridiculous,' Claire said.

'The ice cream? Lunch? Or are you telling me that you don't want to be the Wish Fairy?'

Oh, fudge, here comes the smile again…

'I thought it was your aim in life to wave a wand over everyone and make their dreams come true.'

'If I wave it over the rose garden will you send away the contractor?'

'You can try.'

Alice caught up with them, walking carefully as she carried a little cardboard tray supporting their ices. Hal took one and offered it to her. There was a momentary collision of fingers, fuelling the little personal volcano inside her. The ice should have melted on the spot.

He took one for himself, accepted his change, then, admiring the traffic-light coloured nightmare that would have her daughter spinning like a top, said, 'That looks interesting.'

Resisting the urge to snatch it out of Ally's hand, she bit off the top of the chocolate flake on her own ice. Seeing her spin and whoop, even if it was an additive-induced high, had to be better than the misery of the last week or two.

'Rose gardens, dog walkers, donkeys,' Hal said as he steered her along the bank in Ally's wake until they reached a bench.

'What are you talking about?'

'Magic-wand time. You appear to have a soft spot for dog walkers, donkeys, even teddy bears.'

'Especially teddy bears,' she said, sitting down on a bench strategically placed so that two weeping willows offered a theatrical view of the river. A stage set with brief walk-on parts by passing swans, oarsmen, a passenger boat on its way up-river to Melchester.

'Everyone, in fact, except me.'

CHAPTER NINE

HAL sat down next to her, stretching out in the sunshine, crossing his long legs at the ankles.

'You've got a wish in return for your sponsorship. Just say the word and I'll do my best to deliver.'

He turned his head, regarding her from beneath heavy lids. 'Anything?' he asked.

'Anything that's legal, honest and decent,' she replied to what was clearly a loaded question. 'Or have you already got what you wanted?' she asked. 'Me, sidelined.'

'You're not being sidelined, Claire,' he said, taking the chocolate flake out of his ice, using it to scoop out a dollop of ice cream, sucking it clean, then biting a chunk off the end. 'On the contrary. You are going to be centre stage, making Maybridge a better place to live. Isn't that what you wanted? What your teddy bears picnics and public footpaths are all about?'

She dragged her eyes away. 'All I want,' she said,

'is for you to accept the responsibility that goes with owning a great estate. And the Wish Fairy, as I'm sure you know, is a role for an intern.' Which was true. 'At least the dressing up bit. The features editor usually coordinates the whole thing and some pretty young thing fresh out of school and happy to make a fool of herself in return for getting her picture in the paper, dons the wings and sprinkles fairy dust.'

'You don't do fun?' he asked, watching Ally as, lolly in one hand, she gathered up sticks to drop in the river for a game of Poohsticks around the willow.

'No. Yes! What's that got to do with it? This is my career. I have to be taken seriously.'

'Do you? Always?' He propped an elbow on the back of the bench and turned to face her, his light eyes thoughtful.

'That was the plan, but once I'm in a tutu and wings with all my cellulite on show, there isn't a chance in hell of anyone treating me as anything but a joke.'

'Whatever happened to that little girl who yearned for a red-leather skirt, Claire?'

'The same thing that happened to the boy who rode up the steps of the Hall. She grew up and sadly, a knicker-skimming leather skirt isn't a great look once you've outgrown size zero.'

'You'd still look good in one.' He sucked, thoughtfully, on the ice. 'Perhaps not red.'

'It has to be red. That's the whole point of inappropriate clothing. It has to make the grown-ups tut.' The whole point of inappropriate behaviour, she thought, remembering the barely understood longing to be the girl at the bus stop with Hal North's arm around her.

This brand new desire to be anywhere with Hal North's arm around her. Here, now...

She didn't need her mother to warn her that he was just as dangerous now as he'd always been. More so. Back then she'd been too young, beneath his notice. Now...

From the first moment she'd set eyes on him there had been a frisson of awareness, a quickening that provoked this need to challenge him, make him look, make him see her. And he was here, she was here, sitting beside the river on a sunny day, eating ice cream.

'Growing up,' he said, 'how we all longed for it. The freedom to do what we wanted, be whoever we wanted. We had no idea how lucky we were, wasting precious time before life became all about responsibility with no time to kick back, goof off.'

'You don't become a millionaire by fooling around.' She never doubted that those threads of silver amongst the near-black hair had been hard-earned. She wasn't the only one who'd missed out on playtime. 'What would you do, Hal? If you could goof off for just one day.'

'You know. You were there, remember?'

'Taking a motorcycle to bits?'

'Putting it back together. Riding over the sand-pits on the far side of the Cran.'

'Idiot.'

'I tickled a trout this morning. It's years since I've done that but I had it there between my hands, purring with pleasure before I let it go.'

'Really? Can you really do that?'

'Want me to teach you how?' he asked and her heart rate seemed to slow to match the way a smile moved across his face. The slow-motion deepening of the creases bracketing his mouth, straightening of his lips, lifting of hard cheekbones. The faintest contraction of lines fanning out from eyes that gleamed with a dangerous light. The kind of smile that could burn a woman who didn't have an asbestos guard around her heart. A warning that they were no longer talking about fish.

'I thought it was just a tall story, a fisherman's yarn,' she said.

'You have to know where the fish hide, stand perfectly still, be endlessly patient.'

And in her mind's eye she could see herself standing in the shallow water, Hal behind her, his arms around her as he guided her...

'You stroke them so gently that they don't know you're there. Mesmerise them with your touch, make them want more...'

'I hate fish,' she snapped, as her hormones jangled, uncomfortably, certain now that he wasn't talking about any old trout. 'Ally, be careful!' Hal caught her arm, keeping her at his side when she would have leapt up to pull her away from the bank. 'She'll fall in,' she protested.

'It's shallow and I'm watching her. She won't come to any harm.'

'She'll get wet.'

'It's warm. She'll soon dry off.'

'Are you suggesting that I'm an overprotective mother?' she said stiffly.

'Only because you are an overprotective mother,'

he replied. 'It's understandable, but you need to fight it.'

'Why? What do you know about it?' she demanded, as she watched her daughter, ice lolly in one hand, Poohsticks in the other teetering on the edge as she leaned over to drop them in. 'I would never have been allowed...' She would never have been allowed to get that close to the water, to risk getting her feet wet, mud on her clothes when she'd been Ally's age. She caught herself. 'I'm responsible. She has no one else.'

'Relax,' Hal said softly and she felt the tension flow from her limbs.

She forced herself to take her eyes off Alice for the merest second.

'Don't do that! I'm not one of your blessed fish!'

'No.' What was that expression? Sympathy? She didn't need that. No... It was something else, something she couldn't quite put her finger on.

'It's hard to be everything. Everywhere. To keep her safe. I want so much for her...'

'Take care you don't turn into your mother, Claire.'

'What?' His words were like a slap, the shock of it taking the breath from her body, pushing her to her feet. 'Never!'

'I wonder if Alice ever longs for a red-leather skirt?' Hal sucked a smear of ice cream from his thumb with mesmerising slowness. She wanted to look away, couldn't... 'What does she dream about? Do you know? Have you ever asked her? Did your parents ever ask you?'

'Parents do what they think is best for their child,' she said, aware that she was on the defensive, that she knew too little about what her child was thinking. What was making her unhappy.

'Do they?'

'Mine did everything they could for me.'

'Lucky you.' He crunched up the remains of his ice. 'But even with the best of intentions they don't always get it right. How did they respond to Alice's arrival?'

Feeling rather stupidly way up on her high horse, she sank back onto the bench. 'My dad died a week before Ally was born.'

'Bad timing.'

She sighed. 'Is there a good time to die?'

'In bed at the end of a life well lived?'

'Yes, well, his was cut short by pancreatic cancer. Two years—' chemo, remission, more chemo '—it took two years. He kept working until weeks before the end,' she said. 'Refused to rest. He said he'd have all the time in the world for that.'

He didn't say he was sorry, but then her father had always been on his case. Had, it seems, been the one to deliver his banishment. What threat had he used to keep him away from his home? From his mother? It would have had to be something big.

His stepfather's job? The cottage had been tied to the job and while he might not have cared about the drunk everyone assumed was his father, Hal's mother would have suffered if he'd been sacked.

She was used to asking questions, it was her job, but she wasn't sure she wanted to know the answer to that one. She wanted, needed, to remember her dad as the one person in the world who'd under-stood her. Who'd loved her enough to stand by her when she'd most needed support.

'It must have been hard for you,' Hal said.

She tore her anxious gaze from Ally to glance at him. 'Harder on my dad. And my mother, too. I was able to escape, have fun, if only for a while.'

'With Ally's father?'

She swallowed hard. 'Yes.'

'Don't blame yourself for that.'

'Easier said than done.' It wasn't the fact that she was out having fun while they were suffering. It was the lifetime that came after. 'I have to live with them knowing that I'd lied about where I was, who I was meeting. Letting down parents who only wanted the best for you.'

'I never had that problem.' He finished his ice. 'The house went with the job, of course.'

'Yes…' She wanted to ask him about his childhood. How he'd suffered at the hands of a drunk who wasn't his father. Had he known? His expression suggested not and she said, 'Sir Robert offered my mother the chance to buy the house, my father was well insured, but she didn't want to stay.'

'While you, I imagine, wanted to be close to Ally's father.'

'It wasn't that.' She pulled a face. 'Jared was long gone, but I chose my baby over the future my mother had worked so hard to give me.' She watched Ally, hopping about, happy to be outside, playing. 'Morning sickness instead of a gap year with all those influential friends I'd made at Dower House. She couldn't forgive me for throwing all that away. Or for the fact that my dad had sided with me.'

'He was dying,' Hal said. 'That tends to focus the mind on what's important.'

'Yes.'

So few people had understood. Her mother, her teachers, her friends had all urged her to cut free, take her starred As and fly away from Cranbrook, out into the big wide world.

Her dad had been the only one who'd understood why she'd clung so desperately to a life she had made with love, with passion. A life she was responsible for. A life she had been given in return for the one she was about to lose.

Unexpectedly, Hal did, too.

Working with Hal North Rule Number Seven: Expect the unexpected.

'It couldn't have helped that Alice's father came from a different ethnic background,' he said.

'I met Jared at a party thrown by one of the girls at school. He was at university with her brother and quite the most beautiful man I'd ever seen. Golden, gentle.'

'And gone.'

'He really was desperately sorry when I told him that I was pregnant. And generous.'

'He supports Alice?'

'No…' She broke off, unable to say the words.

'He gave you money to make the problem go away?'

Something in his voice made her look up. 'He

was going home to an arranged marriage. He thought I'd understood that our romance was no more than… Well, you get the picture.' She shrugged. 'I told him I understood, took the money he offered and he flew home assuming that I had used it for the purpose intended.'

'Is that what you used to improve the cottage?'

She shook her head. 'I put it into a fund for Ally. She'll need it when she's older.'

'Mothers…' He shook his head. 'Does she know? Who her father is?'

'Of course. I've kept photographs for her and we put together an impressive family tree when they did an ancestry project at school last term. Jared al Sayyid came from a rich and powerful Ras al Kawi family. Her great-great-great grandfather was a tribal leader who fought with Lawrence. I found loads of photographs on the Net…'

She stopped, frowned.

'What's the matter?'

'What? Oh, nothing. I was just wondering if that could have been the trigger for whatever happened at school.'

'The Arab connection?'

'No,' she said, shocked. 'It's just, well, Ally can be a bit of a drama queen and she did get rather

carried away with the whole Arabian Nights thing.
A bit princessy. It doesn't take much for the pack
to turn on you...'

'It doesn't take much for it to blow over, either.'

'No. Just something to break the ice.' But what?
The longer it went on the harder it became...

'Came?' Hal prompted, as if he'd said it more
than once. She looked at him, confused. 'You
said her father came from a powerful family. Past
tense.'

'Oh, yes. Jared was killed in a car accident a year
after she was born. I wouldn't have known, but it
happened on the Melchester bypass. He was vis-
iting the brother of my school friend... It was one
of the first news items that crossed my desk when
I started at the *Observer*.'

'You weren't tempted to contact his family?'

She shook his head. 'He didn't want that, Hal.
I was something separate, never part of his real
life. Just a few wild oats sown, rather carelessly,
before he married the bride chosen for him by his
family.' She looked across the grass at her long-
limbed daughter. 'Keeping Ally was my decision.
One that I never for a moment regretted.'

For some reason, that made him smile.

'So, your mother left Cranbrook and you moved into my mother's cottage. Extraordinary.'

'There was nothing extraordinary about it. It was empty, I needed somewhere to live.'

'No...' He shook his head. 'You don't see your mother?'

'Not much. She remarried quite soon after she moved and she's busy with her new family.' She dug out a tissue, wiped her fingers. Glanced at her. 'Now you know all my secrets.'

'I doubt that.'

'More than most.' She looked across at him, still stretched out, totally relaxed while she was as taut as a bow spring. 'Now it's your turn to tell me one of yours.'

'Payback time?' he asked, unconcerned.

'Absolutely,' Claire said. 'I tell you mine, you tell me yours. It's only fair.'

'I think the word you're looking for is "show,"' he said. 'As in I show you mine... Or didn't you play that game?' Then, having extracted a blush from her, he said, 'I've already told you my biggest secret.'

She wasn't falling for that.

'That was no more than a distraction. Ancient history. What about now? I know you were married to Suzanne Parsons. Do you have any children?' She had been thinking particularly about Bea Webb's little girl, but afraid she had betrayed too much personal interest she quickly added, 'Where did you go when you left here? How did you turn a motorcycle courier service into an global business? What are you going to do with Cranbrook Park?'

Burying the big question in a heap of little ones. Except that none of them were little.

'Is that it?'

'No, but it will do to be going on with.'

'I don't doubt it. I'd be interested to find out how you found out about Suzanne. It hardly made a blip on the emotional radar.'

'Sorry, that's a professional secret.' She still felt uncomfortable about the way she'd drawn the information from staff who clearly adored him. 'How did you meet her?'

'She worked in the office. Ran the office for me when things started to take off. We were both working crazy hours and had no time for a social life. It just happened but all we had was work and sex. Mostly work. Looking back, I don't even know why we got married,' he said, taking her by surprise. She'd expected him to stonewall her, as he usually did, but maybe he took her demand for a secret seriously.

'It's what they call a starter marriage.'

He glanced at her. 'A what?'

'You know, like a starter home. Small, temporary, a practice run. Somewhere to find out what you really want,' she said.

'Right. Well, Suz has got that sorted. Good bloke who's never been on a motorbike, a couple of kids. Just as well we didn't make that mistake. You can't have starter children,' he said, standing up. 'Shall we walk off those ices?'

'Good plan. Ally!'

There was a smear of mud on one cheek, a dribble of something green on her cardigan and her foot was wet, a total mess. Her mother would be appalled.

'We're going for a walk. There are swings over there.'

'I'm a bit old for swings.' Then with a casual shrug, she said, 'although they're quite big.'

Claire couldn't stop herself from grinning as she walked nonchalantly over to the nearest one and began to gently sway backwards and forwards as if she was just sitting there.

'Will you need a push?' Hal asked.

Ally gave him a pitying look. 'I don't think so,' she said, before letting rip to show him that she was capable of swinging herself, thank you very much.

'You haven't been tempted to try again? Marriage?' she asked, anything to distract herself as Ally swung higher and higher. She would not call out, tell her to be careful…

'Marriage takes commitment, time, if you're going to do it properly,' he said. 'Sex is simpler. What about you?'

'Do I find sex simple?

He didn't answer and she turned to see what he was looking at.

Her.

He was looking at her and for a moment she was back on that roller coaster again, teetering on the edge under the intensity of a gaze that stirred the yearning empty ache low in her belly.

'Well? Do you?'

'Who has the time?' she said, abruptly, turning to look at the restaurant, anywhere but at him.

Built in the early years of the twentieth century as a summerhouse for boating parties from a grand estate on the far side of the river, it resembled an ornate, bamboo birdcage and was a popular spot on a sunny day, even mid-week.

Hal grabbed the chance to take a mental step back.

What the hell was he doing? His reaction to that headline had been to yank her out of the newsroom, turn her into that cartoon. Put her on display for once and see how she liked it.

Instead they were sharing confidences. And he was thinking the unthinkable about the last woman on earth he'd ever date.

'The terrace is beginning to fill up, I'd better grab a table,' he said, leaving her to gather up Ally. Give himself a moment to cool off, although short of a plunge in the river there wasn't much chance of that.

Hal handed each of them a menu when they joined him.

'Could I have a burger?' Ally asked him. 'One with cheese and all that other stuff?'

He looked at Claire.

'If that's what you want,' she said, avoiding his gaze.

'All that other stuff apart from the pickle.'

'Got it,' he said.

'And fries.'

'A burger with cheese and all that other stuff apart from the pickle and fries,' Claire said. 'Anything else?'

'Cola? I don't want a straw.'

'Make that two burgers,' she said, without even looking at her menu. 'One with everything, one without the pickle, both with fries and a cola.'

'Can I go and look at the aviary?' Ally said, already fidgeting to be off.

'Stay where I can see you.'

'Righto!' She beamed a smile at him and then ran over to the aviary that was attached to the restaurant.

'Relaxed enough for you?' Claire asked.

He shook his head. 'I'm shocked. No attempt to steer Ally towards a healthier option? A jacket potato, water instead of cola? Whatever happened to responsible parenting?'

'She gets that twenty-four seven. Everyone needs a break.'

'Your mother would not approve.'

'I know,' she said, and without warning grinned, nearly blowing his socks off. 'I'm overwriting my memory's hard drive.'

'Was your birthday party that bad?'

'I was allowed to invite five carefully selected

school friends. We all wore our best frocks and sat at a table with a white damask cloth and silver cutlery. Tea consisted of tiny cucumber-and-egg sandwiches, scones with clotted cream and pretty little cupcakes. We were allowed cordial, tea or milk to drink.'

'Sweet.'

She pulled a face.

'I was eight not six. I wanted a party at a burger bar. Fast food, fizzy drinks and giggling over absolutely nothing. And jeans. I wanted to wear blue jeans but my mother thought they were common.'

'No red-leather skirt, no blue jeans. Your life was blighted.'

'I was teased rotten about it for weeks afterwards. Little girls can be cruel.'

'Big girls can be cruel, too.'

That had been heartfelt and Claire, who'd been keeping an eye on Ally, gave Hal her full attention.

He'd brushed off his failed marriage, but clearly it hadn't been as simple as he'd made it sound. A man like Hal didn't commit without giving something of himself.

As if conscious of having revealed more than he intended, Hal pulled out the chair next to him.

'You'll be more comfortable if you sit here.

You won't have to keep turning around to check on Ally.'

He was right, but sitting opposite him was bad enough. Looking at him was bad enough. Sitting close enough for their knees to touch, to smell his skin, was more than flesh could stand.

'No. It's fine,' she said. 'You're her new best friend. You watch her while I relax.'

'Three large burgers, hold the pickle on one, all with fries and colas,' he said to the waitress. 'We'll be over by the aviary.' Then when she'd gone he said, 'It's a shame you're not wearing jeans. We'll have to come again and do a thorough job.'

Working with Hal North Rule Number Eight: He can read your mind.

'Coming?' he asked, pushing back his chair. 'Just in case your little animal-rights warrior takes it into her head to set the birds free.'

'No danger. The aviary is glass fronted.'

Ally looked up as they joined her. 'What's that bird?'

'It's a lovebird,' Hal said.

'It looks lonely.'

'You're right. There should be a pair.'

'Like in the Ark… We've got two cats but they're both boys. Tom and Jerry. They're brothers so it would have been cruel to separate them. Do you have any pets, Mr North?'

'Why don't you call me Hal?' he suggested.

'Do you have any pets, Hal?'

'I've got a donkey. His name is Archie.'

'Oh, I know Archie. Mum takes him apples so that he doesn't chase her,' she said, dismissively. 'Have you got a dog?'

Hal, gallantly, responded to the cue. 'Do you like dogs?'

'I love them, but mummy is at work all day so we can't have one.'

'Well, that's a shame, but she's right, they're not like cats. Dogs need people.'

'Sometimes people need dogs. Seeing-eye dogs,' she said, 'hearing dogs, guard dogs. Just-for-company dogs.'

'Do you know, Alice, I was thinking only this morning, when I went for a walk, that I really needed a just-for-company dog. Would you help me to choose one?'

'A puppy?'

'I was thinking that I might go to the animal-rescue centre and see if there was a dog who didn't have a home. I'm sure that's what your mother would suggest.' He looked across Ally's head at her. 'Shall we go after lunch? See what they've got.'

Ally, unaware of the subtext, looked up. 'Can we, Mum? Pleeease.'

'I should be working.'

'Consider it a research trip,' he suggested. 'I'm sure the animal-rescue centre is in need of a wish.'

'What they need,' she said, 'is a wood. So that the teddies can have their picnic.'

'Sorry, I can't help you there. The tree surgeons will be surveying the woods next week, and then they'll be making if safe.' She stared at him. 'You wouldn't want a rotten branch falling on someone's precious Steiff, would you?'

CHAPTER TEN

'Hi, Claire, hi Ally. How are Tom and Jerry? I hope this visit doesn't mean—'

'No, they're fine, Jane. I've brought along my neighbour. He's just moved to the country and he's looking for a dog. Ally is going to help him choose.'

'Well, excellent.' Jane kinked a 'nice one' eyebrow in her direction and she shook her head quickly, smiling when Hal glanced round, clearly picking up the fact that signals were passing between them. 'What sort of dog did you have in mind, Mr—?' Jane said quickly.

'Just call me Hal,' he said.

'Hal.'

She smiled at him. Everyone smiled at him, Claire thought. The waitress at the Birdcage, women having lunch there, Willow and Ally. Especially Ally. Hell, she had smiled at him herself as he'd entertained them effortlessly over lunch. And not just smiled, she'd laughed and for the life of her couldn't have said why, or what they'd talked about. She'd just felt relaxed, happy, hadn't thought once about grilling him…

'Something man-size?' Jane guessed.

'It's not the size, it's the character,' he said. 'But it has to be well behaved. I don't have time to rehabilitate a neurotic dog.'

Jane looked doubtful. 'Dogs are full-time companions. We're very careful where we re-home them,' she warned. 'You do have a garden? Good fences?'

'Hal has plenty of room,' Claire assured her. 'And there's always someone around.'

'Well, good,' she said, reassured. 'Why don't you give him the tour? I've got something special to show Ally.'

Ally hesitated, clearly torn.

'Don't worry, Alice, I won't choose anything until you've given your approval,' Hal said.

'You will regret that,' Claire said, as he stood back to allow her to lead the way.

'Probably, but you know what they say, a man with a couple of hundred acres, must be in want of a dog. Possibly two.' He put his hand on her shoulder and eased her through the door to the kennels. Left it there, a warm, unaccustomed weight that she wanted to lean into. 'Thanks for not ratting on me about the state of my fences.'

'Penny told me that you've got her husband laying hedges. You're obviously giving the estate a thorough overhaul. You could have told me about the woods.'

'You could have looked. A journalist would have checked her facts and seen for herself that it's in a shocking state.'

'My mistake. But I haven't got it wrong about the dog. I know you'll be a responsible owner.'

'Do you? How?'

'You had a dog when you were young. It stuck to you like glue and never put a paw out of place. A cross of some sort. A bit of lurcher, a bit of retriever?'

'The perfect poacher's dog.' He smiled at the memory. 'I haven't had one since Paddy died.'

They stopped at the first kennel. A rough-coated Jack Russell with a black patch over one eye looked up, sat up, grinned, his tongue hanging out.

'Cute,' Claire said, 'but they will dig holes. Murder on the garden.'

'Who'd notice a few more holes in mine except the rabbits?'

'That's just showing off,' she said, digging him in the ribs with her elbow.

He grinned. 'Maybe.'

'The rabbits would undoubtedly prefer if you gave him a miss.'

'Don't they dig up your garden? Eat your lettuce? Plunder your carrots?'

'You appear to be confusing me with Mr McGregor. Fortunately the cats keep Peter Rabbit and his cousins at bay.'

'They have to sing for their supper?'

'We all have to do that.' She hesitated. 'Does the rose garden come under the not-talking-to-the-press rule?'

'I don't think I'll be able to get away with that. Not if I do what you suggest.'

'No. But it would be the garden, the roses that people would be interested in.'

'On that understanding, I might be persuaded to let you cover the restoration in your Greenfly blog,' he said.

His hand on her shoulder had drawn her in and as she turned to look at him, she discovered that he was close enough for her to see the fine stubble on his chin, a small scar that ran across his cheekbone, the individual threads of silver running through his hair at the temples.

If she said 'it's a deal,' would he seal it with a kiss?

'It's a deal.'

'You're teasing me about the bedding plants,' she said quickly.

'Possibly,' he said, turning to the spaniel in the next kennel. His muzzle was turning grey and he rolled his eyes at them, sighed and didn't bother to get up.

A large cream Labrador ambled over to give them a friendly sniff, offer an ear to be scratched. A German Shepherd flung himself in desperation at the bars, a mongrel raised his eyes from a bone to growl a warning and something that looked as if it had had a brush with a French Bulldog rolled onto his back, inviting a tummy rub.

'Have you seen anything you like?' Jane asked, as they returned to the office having looked at a couple dozen dogs of all shapes and sizes.

'How can anyone choose? I feel a heel for not taking them all,' he told her.

'Everyone feels like that, but you mustn't feel guilty. You're doing a good thing just giving one of them a home.'

'Tell us about the Labrador,' Claire said. She'd seen the way he'd lingered, rubbed the dog's ears.

'Bernard. He's three years old, lovely temperament. Health certificate. His owners split up, moved from a house into flats.' She shook her head. 'We see it all the time.'

'You've got me,' Hal said, 'but I need Alice's approval.'

'Ally, you're wanted,' she called, pushing open a door to reveal her sitting on the floor with two tiny white puppies in her lap. Their mother, a West Highland terrier, was keeping an anxious eye on her.

'Look, Mum! Hal! Aren't they just too sweet!'

'The mother was found abandoned,' Jane explained. 'Only two of the puppies survived.' Then, catching sight of Claire's expression. 'Don't worry, they won't be going anywhere until they're weaned.'

'But they will stay together,' Ally insisted, anxiously.

There was an awkward moment of silence, then Hal said, 'Of course they will.' He turned to Jane. 'If I take the whole family, can they come home with me now?'

'You'll take all three? But I thought you wanted the retriever?'

'Him, too.'

'Really?' She was clearly torn between elation and concern. 'You do understand that even with Claire vouching for you we will have to come and check to make sure your home is suitable. Four dogs…'

'Of course.' He took out his wallet and handed her a card. 'How soon can you come?'

Jane looked at the card. Frowned. 'North? You're Henry North? Of Cranbrook Park?'

'Jane…' Claire began, but instead of telling this picnic-cancelling piece of work how he could get off thinking he could take her precious dogs, Jane was beaming up at him.

'Why on earth didn't you say who you were? How lovely to meet you in person. I can't tell you how grateful we are. So generous… And if there's anything we can ever do for you.'

'Actually,' he said, 'maybe there is. I'm looking for a companion for my donkey. What do you advise?'

'Well, now…'

* * *

'Four dogs and a one-eyed pony?' Claire shook her head. 'Are you quite mad?'

'Possibly. In fact this is where I'm going to have to play my personal Wish card.'

'Oh?'

'The terrier and her pups are going to need more time than I can give them until they're free-range, so I'm going to ask Alice to take care of them for me until they're weaned.'

'Ally?'

She looked across at Ally, who was talking to the puppies, already half in love with them. Half in love with this big man who had bought her ice cream and burgers and had made her day shine brighter with his attention, listening to her, encouraging her to chatter away.

Made her day shine brighter…

'No. Please don't do that, Hal, it'll break her heart when she has to give them up.'

He looked at her for a moment as if searching for something in her face, her expression, then, without turning away, said, 'Alice? Your mother is going to be working from home for the next few weeks so I'm leaving the terriers with you to take care of for a while. Can you handle that?'

'Oh, wow!' she said, completely losing her cool in her excitement.

'What on earth do you think you're doing?' she muttered.

'She'll enjoy looking after them.'

'Bastard!' she said under her breath.

'Obviously.'

No! Oh, God, bad word choice but he knew what she meant…

'What will you do with them, with Bernard, once you've made your plans, the Hall is a fancy hotel or conference centre—'

'Both.'

'—and you've gone back to your London penthouse?'

'For a clever woman, you can be remarkably stupid,' he said and there was a moment of utter stillness before he shrugged. 'Obviously Jane will find good homes for them when the time comes.'

Stupid. Got it in one. She'd allowed him to draw her in. Worse, draw in Ally, and this was the result. One nasty headline that she hadn't even written repaid in full.

'Well? Are you going to rush back and tell her not to let me have them?' he asked. 'After your glowing reference?'

'I ought to.' But then she would be the one who'd break Ally's heart. But she would, anyway...

'I thought not. Do you want to bring that box?' he prompted, before encouraging the Lab to jump up into the back of the Range Rover.

She picked up the box containing the leads and dog food he'd bought from Jane and put it beside Bernard, rubbing the Lab's silky ears to reassure him while Hal settled the basket of heartbreak beside Ally on the back seat.

'These dogs are going to need names,' Ally said.

'You're right. Why don't you make a list,' Hal suggested, 'and we'll choose tomorrow. I'll send a box for the pony, Jane,' he called, ignoring her, leaving her to climb aboard by herself and deciding to concentrate on Ally and the terriers when they got home.

'Hal...'

'We'll discuss the Wish-scheme tomorrow,' he said, finally deigning to notice her once the dogs were settled to Ally's exacting standards. 'Is nine o'clock too early for you?'

'I'm sure you'll knock loud enough to wake me if I oversleep,' she replied, matching the chill in his voice and lowering it ten degrees.

'Count on it.'

She heard him say goodbye to Ally, the sound of his footsteps rounding the cottage, the Range Rover turning in the lane and then the snuffling of the dogs.

'Ally, love, leave the puppies to rest now,' she said.

'Alice.'

'Sorry?'

Ally looked up from the basket. 'Hal calls me Alice.'

She'd noticed. 'But Ally is short for Alice Louise.'

'I know, but Alice is more grown up.'

Okaaay... 'Well, Alice Thackeray, it appears that the incredibly clever Hal North has driven away with the dog food, so we're going to have to walk to the village shop and fetch some.'

'Will they be all right on their own?'

'The mother has water—' she should be grateful that he'd remembered to bring in the dishes '—and the cats have had a look and decided the dogs are beneath them, so I think they'll be okay for half an hour. In fact they could probably do with a little peace and quiet after all the excitement.'

She certainly could.

No such luck. Jessie Michaels was at the post-office counter with Savannah. She had to find a way to talk to the woman, try and sort things out, but the village shop wasn't the place for it.

She handed Ally some dog food and headed for the counter, hoping to get away without the girls having to confront one another.

'What's this, Ally?' Mrs Chaudry, who'd known her all her life was looking at the can. 'Have you got a dog now?'

'Actually,' she said, in a clear, carrying voice, no doubt meant for Savannah's ears—so much for discretion, 'I've got three. A mummy dog and her two tiny, tiny puppies.' She cupped her hands to show how little they were. 'They're white and fluffy and totally gorgeous.'

Out of the corner of her eye, she saw Savannah turn and look, unable to resist the magic word—puppies.

'How lovely. What are they called?'

'They don't have names yet. I'm going to make a list when I get home and Hal and I are going to choose tomorrow. I'll get Mum to take a picture on her phone and we'll show you next time we come to the shop.'

'I can't wait.'

Claire, seeing Savannah edge a little closer, backed off and went to pick up a loaf she didn't need. As she turned, she caught Jessie Michaels watching the two girls standing side by side now, but ignoring one another, each waiting for the other to speak first.

Claire headed towards the freezer to give them space. Jessie, taking the hint, followed.

'How is she?' she asked anxiously.

'Alice? Fed up, bored, missing Savannah.'

'Girls… They get cliquey. Silly. Small things get blown up out of all proportion.'

'What was it, do you know?'

She shrugged awkwardly. 'Apparently Ally told everyone that her father was a sheikh and that made her a princess or something…'

'Oh, good grief. It's my fault. I did go a bit over the top with the ancestry thing,' she admitted.

Attempting to make her father someone who mattered.

'I really wish they wouldn't do that family tree thing,' Jessie said. 'You start digging around in the past and all kinds of stuff comes up that you'd really rather not know about. How have you been coping during half term?'

'My boss has arranged for me to work at home

for a few weeks.' Would she be missed from the news desk? Or once the Wish List thing was done and dusted would they realise that they'd managed perfectly well without her?

They both turned at the sound of a giggle from the counter. The two girls were head-to-head, instant friends again in the way that only children can be. Ally turned to look for her.

'Mum, can Sav come and see the puppies?'

'If her mother says it's all right.' Then she said, 'Maybe she'd like to stay to tea?'

Claire sat at her desk, phone in her hand.

Downstairs the dogs were asleep in their basket. On the floor above her, Alice and Savannah were choosing names for them. She couldn't put it off a moment longer…

She dialled the number of the estate office, the only number that was listed, and wasn't sure whether she was disappointed or relieved when, for once, it was picked up by an answering machine.

There was so much she could say, she thought, as she listened to Penny's voice inviting her to leave a message. So much she should say.

Clearly Hal hadn't forgotten to leave the dog food. He'd known that the puppies would be an irresistible draw to Ally's friends and that if she bought food in the village shop everyone would know about them by the next morning. She just got lucky that Savannah was there...

But she didn't have to say any of those things.

He knew what he'd done and although it had taken her a while to cotton on, so did she and when the beep sounded she kept it short.

Hal paused, looked up from his laptop as the answering machine picked up an incoming call.

'You are too clever by half, Hal North.' Miss Snooty Smartyhat. 'And you're right. I'm stupid. Thank you.'

'Too clever for my own good,' he muttered, reaching to delete the message and instead pressing Play Again.

Bernard lifted his head from his paws and looked at him, his eyebrows poetry in motion.

'What?'

He whined softly, sat up.

'You want me to call her back?' he asked, earning himself a woof of encouragement. The dog had been in the house for no more than three hours and already he thought he owned it. 'The trouble with you Labradors is that you are just so easy,' he said, forcing himself to hit Delete; it wasn't something he wanted Penny to hear when she arrived in the morning. 'You're anyone's for the rub of an ear.'

As for him, easy wasn't the word.

Another thirty seconds and he'd have been hitting Call Back, just to make sure that the puppies had settled, that Alice was coping, to hear her say thank you again in that sweet, musical voice that seemed to whisper over his skin.

His intention had been to give her a hard time, use her newspaper to show her two could play dirty, knowing how much she'd hate dressing up as a fairy, being cut off from the news desk.

Instead, he'd taken her to lunch, lumbered himself with a menagerie and, in the process, had completely forgotten who she was, why he wanted to hurt her, until she'd turned on him.

He had been so sure she'd instantly pick up on what he was trying to do, but he'd seriously underestimated the defence mechanism of the mother defending her young from the possibility of pain.

Stupid. He was the one who was stupid.

How often had his mother stepped between him and Jack North, taken the blows until he'd been big enough to strike back. But then it was Jack his mother had rushed to comfort, bathing his lip, crooning to him.

Bernard pushed impatiently at his hand.

'Behave, or I'll trade you in for that Jack Russell,' he warned, even as his hand rested on Bernard's broad head. 'We both know that if I suggested a good long walk right now you'd forget about Claire Thackeray in a heartbeat.'

Bernard was on his feet and at the door a second after the word 'walk' had left his lips and abandoning his laptop he headed for the mudroom and picked up a lead before following him out into the soft evening. With luck, a walk would have a similarly amnesia-inducing effect on him.

Claire worked late, dealing with comments on her "Greenfly and Dandelion" blog, answering queries.

She had no formal training, did not pretend to be an expert, but her mother had studied garden design at the same college as her father had studied estate management and, between them, she'd absorbed a lot of practical knowledge.

In the period between Ally's birth and the time she started at pre-school, she'd had a lot of time to fill, but no money and she'd put all her efforts into making her home, creating her garden.

Blog done, she sent Brian an update on the teddy bears picnic story—turning Hal North from villain to something more like a hero.

Just because she was off the news desk didn't mean she couldn't contribute. Besides, he was right. She should have looked for a reason.

Cranfield Wood had been hit hard during the storm, but she remembered her dad complaining that there had been no money to restore it. The truth was that it had been neglected for years and it was all about Health and Safety these days.

Was that the problem with the footpath, too?

She would look, she promised herself, turning to the box of her father's things that she'd brought down from the loft. It contained his journals, the photographs he'd taken of the estate and with luck there would be photographs of the damage caused by the big storm back in the nineteen-eighties that she could scan and attach to her piece.

That done, she went on looking, searching for one face. Not Hal, he'd never been in those group shots of beaters, estate workers, but someone else might be there. And she turned the pages long into the night, searching for a resemblance, a clue…

CHAPTER ELEVEN

DESPITE her late night Claire was up at sunrise planting out the summer bedding she'd been hardening off.

There was nothing like back-breaking work to take your mind off the parts that were stirring, demanding some attention.

Fat chance.

Hal had expected her to know what he was thinking and she'd blown it. Well, she'd finally caught on, thanked him and she half expected him to call back and tease her on her slowness. Hoped…

'You're early,' she said, glancing at the clock as, having rapped on the open door, Hal walked in without waiting for an invitation. She'd heard him coming—the gravel made a good burglar alarm—had time to still her beating heart. 'It's only eight-thirty. What's up? No one to keep you in bed?' she asked.

'Sadly, no. Not that it would have mattered one way or the other. The contractors arrived at seven to start emergency work on the roof. If it didn't sound paranoid, I'd swear that Cranbrook sold the lead himself when he knew he'd lose the house.'

'You're right,' she said. 'That does sound paranoid.'

'You didn't see him the day he signed the contract.'

'He was there?' she asked, surprised, a little shocked. 'I heard he'd had a stroke. How was he?'

'In surprisingly good voice,' he said, turning away, looking out of the window. 'The reason I came to knock you up early is because I have another meeting at ten.'

'Sorry, you're hours too late to have that pleasure. Have you had breakfast?' she asked.

'Yes, thanks, but I wouldn't say no to a cup of coffee if there's one going. Is Alice around?'

'Working on a school project. Half-term homework. Just to keep us parents up to scratch.' She switched on the kettle, turned to face him. 'Hal…'

'I got your message,' he said, before she could say any more.

'I'm sorry I was so slow on the uptake,' she said, turning to lean back against the counter, refusing to let him brush the subject aside. 'The puppy wheeze worked a treat but it still doesn't solve the problem of what you'll do with all this livestock when you go back to London.'

'Who said I was going back to London?' he said. And looked as shocked as she felt; almost as if his mouth had bypassed his brain and spoken from some deeper instinctive place.

"The heart has its reasons which reason knows nothing of…"

For some reason the quotation had been running through her head.

'Hello, Hal!'

He turned, almost with relief she thought, as Alice bounced into the room clutching the list she'd been working on.

'Hello, Alice.'

'Excuse me, young lady,' she said, trying very hard not to resent the fact that her daughter had got a much warmer greeting from Hal than she had. That Ally—Alice—had interrupted a moment when he might have said anything. 'You are supposed to be working.'

'I have been working. I've been working for hours,' she said. 'It has to be break time. There are rules about that sort of thing, you know. A children's charter. Human rights, loads of stuff…' She put the sheet of paper on the table, and poured herself a mug of milk, raided the biscuit tin. 'Besides, Hal and I need to settle on some names. We can't go on calling the dogs Mummy Dog, Baby Dog One and Baby Dog Two forever, can we?

'Certainly not. Show me what you've got,' Hal said, pulling out a chair and sitting down.

'Well, I thought we could call the mummy dog Dandelion, because she's all white fluff.'

'I like it.'

She gave him a big smile. 'You could call her Dandy for short.'

'I really like it.'

'And then Savannah and I drew up a list of names for the puppies. I was thinking maybe Thistle for Baby Dog One.'

'Thistle?'

'I was thinking Purple and Prickly,' Claire said, helping him out, 'but apparently we're doing seed heads.'

'So that would be Thistle, short for Thistledown? It works for me,' Hal said.

Well, great…

'Now,' Alice said, 'the next one is a bit tricky. I like Parsley…'

'Parsley?'

'That's cow parsley, of course, not the green

stuff that Mum grows in the herb garden, but Sav wanted Bramble.'

'Savannah is Alice's best friend,' Claire explained. 'She came to tea yesterday. To see the puppies.'

'Bramble flowers are white but there's no fluff,' Alice said. 'Just blackberries.'

'I see your problem.'

'They're doing a wild-flower project this term,' she said, refusing to be ignored. 'Endangered habitats. There are bee orchids, cowslips, fritillary in the long meadow, did you know? We'd have lost them without the rabbits to graze it.'

'It's a good job we didn't go for the Jack Russell, then,' he said, finally raising his head to look at her. There was a moment of connection over a good memory, shared, before he turned back to Alice. 'I really like Parsley, but if it would make Sav happy maybe we should go with her choice.'

'Dandelion, Thistledown and Bramble,' Alice said, ticking their choices. 'Okay. They'll need name tags for their collars. Will you organise that?'

'I'll get it done straight away. Great job, both of you.'

Alice beamed. Then, looking around, said, 'Did you bring Bernard to visit them?'

'No. He's been out for a long walk this morning and decided he'd rather take a nap under Penny's desk.' Seeing her disappointment, he said, 'The pony's arriving after lunch if you want to come up and say hello. You can say hello to Bernard then. Bring Sav, too, if you like.'

'Great. Mum, can I use your computer? I want to look up West Highland terriers, just to make sure I'm doing all the right things.'

'Help yourself.' She poured out a couple of mugs of coffee, sat down. She wanted to thank him again, but it was probably better to stick to business. 'The Wish scheme. Willow said you had some ideas?' she prompted, head down, pen at the ready.

He didn't respond and she looked up.

'I'm really sorry about calling you a bastard.'

'Are you?'

'What will it take to convince you?' she asked and remembered, too late, another moment when she'd said that. Another moment, right here in this kitchen, when he'd told her that her mouth would get her into trouble.

Hal's face was giving her no clues as to what was going through his mind, but if she had to gamble, she'd have said that he was thinking much the same thing.

He held her gaze for a moment that seemed to stretch like an elastic band, with the same breath-holding uncertainty about when it would snap.

'I'll let you know,' he said, finally, looking away. 'In the meantime, tell me what you think about a cycle path across the estate. From the village right into the town.'

'A cycle path?' Gratefully seizing the reprieve, she said, 'Where did you have in mind?'

He took a map of the estate from his pocket and unfolded it on the table. 'Here, on the far side of the Cran,' he said and she leaned forward so that she could follow the route he traced with his finger.

'Across here?' she asked.

He looked up, catching the note of confusion in her voice.

'Yes. Do you have a problem with it?'

His eyes were particularly blue this morning, his hair had grown out of the perfect trim and he was beginning to look less like a man who'd strayed from his city office into the country, more like a man who was at home there.

'Claire?'

The lines of his face had relaxed into a smile,

his mouth into the sensuous curve of a man whose thoughts had nothing to do with cycle paths.

He lifted his hand to her cheek, slid his fingers through hair escaping untidily from the band she used to keep it out of her face while she was in the garden, cradled her head. The noises of the countryside drifted in through the open doorway.

A chainsaw whining as it cut through a branch somewhere, a thrush declaring territorial rights, a tractor...

She heard none of them as his lips touched hers. All her senses were concentrated on Hal. On the touch of his fingers, entangled in her hair, on the taste of toothpaste, fresh and sharp against her mouth, the scent of his skin... He'd come to her fresh from the shower after his early walk.

Her lips parted of their own volition, her tongue teased gently inside his lip and there was nothing in the world but the two of them as he kissed her, sweetly, thoroughly, with total conviction until a thud from the room above brought them crashing back to their senses.

'Okay,' he said casually, 'we'll call that a down payment. Now, you will please concentrate on the cycle path.'

He had to be kidding...

'What, exactly, is your problem with the route?'

She blinked, swallowed. Concentrate? He expected her to concentrate when he was still looking at her as if...

'A down payment!'

'I'm almost convinced,' he said, 'but your apology still needs a little work. Now the cycle path?' he prompted, as if what had happened was the most ordinary thing in the world. Maybe, almost certainly, for him it was...

Focus, Claire!

'I don't have a problem with it,' she said, doing her best to be as blasé as Hal. 'It's perfect except...'

What?

There had been something and she dragged her gaze from his, looked at the map. The route. Oh, yes...

'What about your golf course?' she asked.

'What golf course?'

'Isn't there going to be a golf course for your hotel and conference guests?'

'I hope not. I've earmarked the sandpits area as a scramble course where local lads can let off steam on their motorbikes in safety. Learn maintenance. There's a keeper's hut up there that would make a good clubhouse. It's on my list of ideas for the town to vote on.'

'And if they don't like it?'

'I'll do it anyway.' He waited. 'And the cycle path?'

'Is a brilliant idea. The kids could ride in safety to the high school instead of catching the bus. I could ride safely to work. If I was going to work.' She paused. 'If I had a bike.'

'Well, um, great. So, which one is going to be your personal "Wish"?'

'Neither. I want the town to approve of the scramble club, and the cycle path is a public amenity. If they want, they should put in a bit of effort. My personal "Wish" is for help to restore the temple beside the lake.'

'Oh.'

'I'm getting that look,' he said. 'The one that says I can afford to pay someone to do it.'

'Well, you can. At least I'm hoping you can, because that's going to be peanuts compared to the cost of repairs and renovations to the Hall with every move monitored by English Heritage. You won't be able to get away with that PVC guttering you've put up at the back of the house.'

'It's temporary. The replacements will have to be specially cast.'

'Good grief. How much will that cost?'

'Not peanuts,' he assured her. 'But it's not about the money. You keep telling me that Cranbrook Park should be available for the community. I think the community should prove that they care about it enough to put something back, don't you?'

'Is Cranbrook Park going to be available for the community?' she asked.

'You're just going to have to trust me on that, Claire,' he said, getting up.

'Like the wood and the puppies and no doubt some perfectly good reason for closing the footpath?'

'Here's my list of project ideas,' he said, placing an envelope on the table. 'Take a look, let me know what you think when you bring the girls up to the Hall this afternoon to meet the pony.'

'I'm included in the invitation?'

'Only if you bring another cake. Gary ate most of the last one.'

She laughed. 'I knew that would get you in the end.'

'You don't know a thing, Claire Thackeray,' he

said, 'or you'd be a lot more worried.' He paused in the doorway. 'There is one more thing.'

She rose slowly to her feet. 'Yes?'

'I have to go to a charity dinner on Saturday night and I need a partner.'

'Dinner…' Was he asking her on a date?

'It's in London,' he warned. 'A black-tie event. Is that a problem?' he asked. Almost as if he immediately regretted mentioning it. Wanted her to turn him down.

She ought to turn him down.

'I may not have fulfilled my potential, Hal, but I do possess a long frock. I bought it cheap in a sale for the *Observer* Christmas party,' she added. 'It's dark blue and everyone wants black.'

'I don't care if you bought it in a charity shop,' he replied. 'I just need someone to fill an empty seat.'

'And having wondered who you knew who wouldn't have a date for Saturday night, you thought of me.'

Sweet.

'Have you?' he asked.

'Got a date? Hold on, I'll check,' turning to unhook the calendar from the kitchen wall,

She knew she should tell him that she was busy. No woman should be free on a Saturday night, it said so in all the dating manuals, but he wouldn't be fooled. She was never going to have a date any night of the week.

The big question was why didn't he have one?

Who cared? When would she ever have another chance to place a tick in her fantasy-date box?

'Well?' he asked impatiently.

'I do have bingo in the church hall pencilled in for Saturday,' she said, 'but you're in luck.'

'You'd give up bingo for me?'

'No, but the village hall had a plumbing disaster last week and it's been cancelled.'

'Can you get a babysitter?'

The single parents' get-out-of-jail-free card. No babysitter, no date…

'I'll let you know.'

'This is my mobile number,' he said, writing it on the back of the envelope. 'Call me.'

She waited for the sound of his feet on gravel, but it didn't come and when she glanced out of the window, she saw him walking through her garden. He stopped in the play area and she half hoped to catch him doing hopscotch. Maybe it was a girl thing…

He took his time, doing a little looking of his

own, before he climbed over the fence and walked up the hill towards the Hall.

Claire filled a bucket with hot, soapy water and sat on the doorstep washing her plant trays. Not until they were spotless and drying in the sun did she get out her phone and call Penny to ask her if she was up for a Saturday night babysitting job.

'You've got a date?' she asked, delighted.

'Oh, no…' She'd been left in no doubt on that score. This wasn't 'convincing' Hal part two—at least not in that way. Her punishment was an evening at a dull dinner that he wasn't going to inflict on any woman he cared about. But one man's punishment was another woman's…research opportunity. 'It's work,' she said.

'Why don't I have a job like that?'

'The thing is, it's going to be a late one. Is that going to be a problem?' Now she was the one sounding as if she was hoping for a reprieve.

'Of course not. Ally can stay over with us. I've got a ton of baking to do for the school Spring Fayre and she can help me.'

'She'll love that except…'

'Yes?'

'She's taking her responsibility for the puppies

very seriously. I think she'll insist on them coming, too.'

'No problem. I might even be tempted to have
one of the puppies if Ally will let them be sepa-
rated.'

'You are a star.'

Hal's phone bleeped, warning him of the arrival
of a text.

Sitter sorted. Time?

Uncharacteristically economical with words
for Claire Thackeray and interesting that she had
texted rather than called him. Could it be that she
was still so mad that she couldn't trust herself to
speak to him?

Or had she picked up on his own uncertainty and
didn't want to risk saying something that would
give him an excuse to change his mind?

He still didn't know why he'd asked her instead
of one of half a dozen women whom he could
have called, who would have been happy to fill
the seat beside him even at such short notice. And
his bed, when the dinner was over, if it was on
offer. Infinitely simpler.

Or maybe he did.

He'd told Claire that sex was simpler than getting involved in an emotional relationship, but it was soulless, too. Little more than going through the motions while his exchanges with Claire raised his pulse, left him wanting more.

Her tongue was sharp but her eyes were soft and her anger was the kind that only needed a touch to explode into rip-your-clothes-off desire. Then there was the added edge in knowing that she wanted something from him. His story. His life. The suspense in wondering how far she'd go to get it.

Would she flutter her eyelashes at him again? Flirt?

Risk another meltdown kiss?

The thought of her touching close in the dark rear of the car, touching close as they sat shoulder to shoulder over dinner, thigh-to-shoulder close as they danced, had him achingly hard. That he was sure she felt the same way lent Saturday night a dangerous, touchpaper volatility that made him feel like the kid that had, once upon a time, run wild in Cranbrook Park.

She might be the last woman on earth he'd ever date, but he hit Reply, thumbed in—6:45 I won't wait.

CHAPTER TWELVE

AT exactly fifteen minutes to seven on Saturday evening there was a long ring on the doorbell.

Claire took a last glance in the hall mirror, checked her hair, pulled on an artfully arranged tendril, putting off the moment for as long as she dared. Then she took a deep breath and opened the door.

The breath wasn't enough. What she needed was a quick blast of oxygen as she got the full effect of Hal North in a dinner jacket. It should be a criminal offence for any man to look that good.

'Ready?' he asked impatiently. Clearly he wasn't reduced to similar gibbering incoherence by the efforts she'd made with her hair, her make-up, her bargain-basement dress. 'No last instructions to the babysitter?'

Dating Hal North Rule Number One: This is not a date.

'Alice and the dogs are having a sleepover with Penny.' She handed him the heavy naval officer's dress cloak that had belonged to her great-grandfather. 'Didn't she tell you?'

'Penny? We don't gossip over the ledgers.'

'Neither do we,' she said, turning so that he put it over her shoulders. 'I would never ask her anything about Cranbrook Park. Or you.'

'Discretion. How rare these days.' His fingers momentarily brushed her naked shoulders as he settled the cloak into place, then, as she turned to face him, he looked her up and down, raised an eyebrow. 'Shouldn't you have a sword to go with that?'

'Yes, but it tends to cause havoc when I'm dancing.'

'Then I'm glad you decided to go unarmed.' He stepped out onto the path, waited while she picked up a small clutch purse, made sure the door was shut, then, with his hand to her back, followed her down the path to the waiting car. 'Who does she think you're with? Penny.'

'I told her it was work.' She smiled at the driver who was holding the door and stepped inside, gathering the cloak around her as she sat down. 'Which of course, it is.'

'If that's a warning that I'm going to be talking

to the press all evening,' he said, sitting beside her, 'this could be a very quiet journey.'

'That would be a pity. Just think of me as your fairy godmother. Which means, unfortunately, that this car will turn into a pumpkin at twelve.'

'That should prove interesting if we're on the motorway at the time.'

'Hopefully it will concentrate your mind,' she said. 'I promised my daughter I wouldn't stay out after midnight.'

'And she believed you?'

'Of course. I'm her mother. So, tell me about this dinner we're going to.'

'It's a charity event. There's going to be an auction to raise funds for the homeless.'

'You should have told me. I didn't bring my chequebook. Just a little emergency money tucked into my underwear.'

'Don't worry,' he replied. 'I'll look away while you retrieve it. If anything catches your eyes.'

'My emergencies don't come that expensive,' she said.

'Well, if anything catches your eye just say and I'll bid for you. You can always settle up later.'

'Thanks. I'll remember that.'

Settle up? There was something about the way he said that…

Dating Hal North Rule Number Two: Sit on your hands.

'And I asked you because I don't go to clubs or parties or any of the places where you meet up with unattached women.' He looked across at her. 'Pretty much like you, I imagine.'

'Oh, I'm not into women.' She raised her hand in a dismissive little gesture. 'Not in that way.'

'I got that impression,' he said. 'Is there a man in your life?'

Weird question. Did he think she would have kissed him like that if she'd had anyone even remotely attached to her? Obviously he did. Which meant that she shouldn't take his kiss too seriously.

'It's Saturday night and I'm out with you filling an empty chair,' she said with what she hoped came across as careless indifference. 'What do you think?'

'I thought we'd already established that for you this is work,' he said. 'As it is for me. You're right, Bea does usually fill in on these occasions but she's started leaving details of dating websites on my desk, so I'm taking the hint that she has better things to do on a Saturday night. Have you ever tried that?'

'Online dating?' She shook her head. 'A colleague persuaded me to go speed dating with her once, but Alice had an earache so I had to miss it.' She sighed. 'I was devastated.' Then, when he didn't respond, she said, 'That was your cue to laugh, Hal.'

'Was it? I appear to be sadly out of practice with this.'

She doubted that. Just as she doubted the fact that his assistant acted as his walker on these occasions. No man as good-looking as Hal North, as rich as Hal North, would ever have to go hunting for a date.

'Your assistant doesn't have to be entertained?' she asked.

'We usually talk about work.'

'No wonder she bailed out,' she said, firmly suppressing a tiny 'hooray.' 'That would be the plummy Ms Webb?' she enquired. He probably had more than one assistant.

'Plummy?'

'Plummy. "Don't you people ever speak to one another?"' she quoted in a particularly rich level of plum. "'I've already told your editor that Mr North does not speak to the press...'"

Her performance earned her an appreciative chuckle.

'That's better.'

'I'm a fast learner.'

'She didn't tell you that I'd called, did she?'

'Maybe she didn't think you were important enough.'

'That was the impression I got.' It was warm in the car and she unhooked the cloak, pushed it back off her shoulders. 'Tell me, Hal, how did you make the leap from a youth with a bad attitude to multimillionaire?'

'You don't subscribe to the subtle school of interview technique do you, Claire? I thought the idea was to put people at their ease, draw them out gradually until they were answering your questions without noticing.'

'Oh, please. That would be a complete waste of time. You're on your guard, waiting for the questions, so I thought I might as well get them out of the way and then we can relax and enjoy ourselves.'

'Good plan. You can tick that one off. How's your foot?' he asked.

'Fully healed, thanks. You give great first aid.'

'No excuse not to dance, then.'

'Dance?'

'I assumed, since you left your sword at home, that it was your intention to tango.'

'I was making conversation,' she squeaked as, for a moment, her carefully worked out plan of attack deserted her and all she could think of was Hal holding her, her hand in his, his hand at her waist, sliding lower as he pulled her close against his hips...

Dating Hal North Rule Number Three: Carry a fan at all times.

'You do dance?' he persisted.

'I may need reminding... How's the pony settling in?' He hadn't been there when she'd taken Alice and Savannah to see him after school. He'd been called away to London according to Penny. Urgent business. How long would he stay?

'Archie is teaching him the ropes. What happened to the cake I was promised?'

'The guys working on the roof had a tea break. Who gave you your start?' she asked.

'My start?'

'In business. There must have been someone.

You can't make the kind of leap you've done without a hand up.'

'I don't recall any hand being involved. Only a metaphorical boot in the backside from your father.' He thought about it. 'Forget the metaphorical.'

She'd hoped that by disarming him with her candour, maybe making him laugh a little, Hal would relent and tell her his story. It wasn't going to happen and bearing in mind that all those girls who'd giggled at the bus stop, who'd called her names, would die to be where she was now, in a limousine, going to a black-tie dinner in London with Hal North, she gave it up.

Instead of worrying about her story she should just seize the moment, enjoy it. And with that decided, she half turned and propped her elbow against the back seat so that she was facing him.

'Okay, here's a novel idea, Hal,' she said. 'Let's call a truce for tonight, forget about the past, the future and simply enjoy ourselves.'

'You're suggesting that we should go for fun?'

If she'd wanted to surprise him, then she'd apparently scored a bullseye.

'Isn't that the idea? Eat a little, dance a little, spend loads of your money on a good cause.'

He shifted in his seat so that he was facing her. 'I notice you didn't say "our" money.'

'We both know that I don't have any, but I'll be cheering you all the way.'

'No past, no future, just the present?'

'Until the clock strikes twelve,' she said, offering her hand to seal the bargain.

'Until midnight, Cinderella,' he said, taking it. 'And this time, let's try to get you home with both shoes.

Claire was wearing her hair pinned up, but not in that frightful schoolmarm way she'd had it when she ridden into him on her bicycle.

It was a tumble of curls from which tendrils escaped to coil softly against her cheek. Her only jewellery was a pair of long dark blue enamelled and silver earrings which drew attention to a neck that begged to be stroked and her dress might have been a bargain but it had the kind of elegant simplicity that emphasized her slender figure, her height. Better still, there were no buttons, just tiny straps which had a tendency to slip off her shoulders when she shrugged in a way that gave a man all kinds of inappropriate ideas.

One slipped now as she laughed at something

her neighbour said to her and she left it dangling, more interested in conversation than clothes. She had been a hit with these people. She talked to the women about the things that interested them, laughed in all the right places. Charmed the men without alienating their wives.

Why was he surprised?

She might not have gone to university but she was well educated, had a job requiring empathy, as well as intelligence.

He would do well to remember the intelligence.

No doubt she was simply biding her time, hoping that he would crumble and reveal some dark secret, but having made her deal, she had thrown herself into the evening with enthusiasm. And just as he had when they'd had lunch together, he'd forgotten who she was.

She turned, caught him looking at her. 'What? Have I got spinach between my teeth?'

'Was there spinach? I didn't notice.' He hadn't been noticing much of anything. All he could think about was holding her as they danced. No... 'Elizabeth was admiring your earrings,' he said. He really mustn't think about holding her. His hand at her back, his body betraying what she did to him. Elizabeth, thankfully, turned at the sound of her name. 'I was telling Claire that you were asking about her earrings.' She'd assumed that he'd bought them for her. And put the idea in his mind of dressing her naked body in jewels… Possessing her.

'Aren't they gorgeous?' Claire said enthusiastically, not girly or coy. 'I wrote a piece about a local jewellery designer for the women's page of my newspaper and I couldn't resist treating myself. Every piece is different,' she said, taking a pen out of her purse to write something on the menu. 'That's her website,' she said, putting her hand on his arm as she leaned across to hand it to the woman.

The move exposed the delicious curve of neck and shoulder and all he could think about was touching his lips to the point where they met, about tasting her skin, sinking his teeth into the smooth flesh and sucking it into his mouth.

Only the sharp rap of a gavel from the television personality conducting the auction saved him from making a complete ass of himself.

'Okay, everyone. We've softened you up with good food and good wine and before we let you loose on the dance floor we're going to part you from your money for a great cause.'

Claire straightened. 'Uh-oh. That's the cue for me to sit on my hands.'

He caught one before she could carry out her threat, wrapping his fingers around it. 'Don't do that. I want you to bid for me.'

'Really?' She sounded wary, but her eyes were sparkling with excitement. 'Suppose I get carried away?'

'That's the whole idea. It's for charity.'

'Okaaay…' She used her free hand to pick up the list of lots to be auctioned. 'What takes your fancy? A sporting trophy for your office wall? A cricket bat signed by the Ashes-winning team?' She looked up and he shook his head. 'Not interested? Maybe something from the world of transport. A spoiler from an F1 car? An early Rolls Royce mascot? Or are you interested in a different kind of trophy?' She grinned. 'How about a bra which was worn by—'

'I don't think it would fit me,' he said.

'It's not to wear, it's to drool over.'

'If I'm going to drool over a bra, Claire, I want the owner to be inside it.'

'Bad luck. I'm not…'

'I know,' he said. And, never taking his eyes from hers, he hooked a finger beneath the strap that had slipped from her shoulder and lifted it back into place.

He had barely touched her and yet every nerve ending was alight with anticipation. How long had it been since he'd felt that way?

Was it the uncertainty? He had done a little research of his own and knew a lot more about Claire Thackeray than she knew about him.

Penny had been a mine of information. Not gossip, but responding to carefully phrased questions she had let slip far more than she knew. An admiring comment about Claire's garden had, for instance, had her waxing lyrical about how she'd transformed the rank half acre of weeds that had been Jack North's legacy into a garden entirely on her own.

And her response to the, 'She must have had help with the heavy work. A boyfriend?' had been a firm negative. Apparently there had been no one. Which made the way she responded to his kisses rare. Real…

Claire shivered.

Hal had barely touched her and yet, as his fingertip brushed the shoulder, her skin had goosed and just the thought of dancing with him had her simmering. Scarcely any wonder that she'd blurted that out about her lack of a bra…

She took a sip of water. Held the glass to her cheek.

Until then she'd been doing so well. Being a good dinner guest, talking to the women, drawing them out—well, it was her job—laughing at the men's jokes when all she'd wanted to do was look at Hal. Lay her fingers on the smooth dark cloth of his jacket sleeve as she leaned a little closer as if to catch what he was saying. To breath in the faint citrus scent of his aftershave.

Dating Hal North Rule Number Four: Do not mention underwear.

Dating Hal North Rule Number Five: Do not mention the fact that you're not wearing a bra…

'When I say I'm not…' she said.

'Lot number one is an England rugby shirt worn by Johnny Wilkinson. Who'll start me off at—'

'Put your hand up, Claire.'

'What?'

'Put it up now.'

'—a thousand pounds. And we have a great starting bid from the lovely lady sitting just below me.'

'No…' She realised that everyone was looking

at her. 'Did he say a thousand pounds?' she asked, snatching her hand down. 'It's not even clean!'

'Don't be shy, gorgeous.' The comedian leaned on the podium. 'Stand up and let everyone see what a generous woman looks like.'

She swallowed, glanced at Hal.

'Do as the man says. Gorgeous.'

'Bastard,' she mouthed as she forced herself up on rubber legs, but this time he smiled.

'What's your name, darling?'

'Claire…' She cleared her throat. 'Claire Thackeray.'

'Well, there you have it. The gorgeous Claire Thackeray has set the benchmark for tonight's auction with an opening bid of a thousand pounds. But you're not going to let her get away with this shirt, this muddy, sweaty shirt straight from the back of one of England's finest for a mere thousand pounds are you ladies?' He put his hand to his ear. 'Are you ladies?'

'Did you enjoy that?' Hal asked, as the bidding raced away and the auction took off.

'Are you kidding?' she demanded. 'Playing patsy to an auctioneer is not my idea of a good time.'

'Someone has to break the ice and we were both

in need of a distraction. It was that or a jug of cold water in my lap.'

So it wasn't just her…

'If that's your problem, Hal,' she said, 'buckle up for an expensive night, because I'm going to have to keep on bidding.'

'I've got a better idea.' He seized her wrist and stood up, attracting the attention of the auctioneer. 'Ten thousand pounds,' he said, heading for the door before the gavel came down.

'Sold to the man exiting left in a hurry with the lovely Claire Thackeray. We'll catch up with you later, Hal!'

'What did you just bid for?' Claire gasped as the lift doors closed on them.

'Who cares?' he said, bracketing her with his arms on the mirrored wall of the lift, his body pinning her against it.

She thought he was going to kiss her, but he didn't. He just held there, her breasts crushed against his chest, his thighs containing her, the tumescent evidence of his need rigid against her abdomen. He held her with his body, with his eyes and the hot, sweet ache of desire surged through her veins, liquefied between her legs…

'But your guests…' she gasped, in a last-ditch attempt at sanity.

'Will have to provide their own distractions. I have to get you home by midnight…'

'We're never going to make it.'

'My home.'

The lift came to a halt, the doors opened, some-one cleared their throat and he must of thought of something very painful to have regained such swift control before he stepped back and, nodding to the couple waiting for the lift, walked her into the foyer where her cloak was produced while she was still fumbling in her purse for the ticket.

He didn't touch her in the taxi that the doorman had waiting, didn't even hold her hand. He didn't touch her in the small lift that whisked them to the top of his riverside apartment block. He didn't have to.

Everything that was between them had been acknowledged, accepted as they'd ridden the lift down from the banqueting suite and now the air was vibrating with something primal, ancient; she was shaking with the need to feel the roughness of his skin against hers, the velvet, the silk, the steel…

Knowing him was her destiny. Here, now was

the moment and when they touched there would be no stopping, no going back.

By the time they'd reached the top floor and the door of the apartment had been kicked shut, every nerve ending was tingling. Her breasts were hard peaks that not even the bra built into her dress could disguise. They demanded to be touched, kissed, pinched. Her body was a melting inferno and she took no more than three paces into the apartment before she turned and let the heavy cloak fall at her feet.

Hal discarded his jacket, took a step towards her, let his hands rest momentarily on her shoulders, his thumbs stroking her neck as his eyes ate her up. She anticipated a fierce hunger, wanted it, was practically screaming for it, but his kiss was the antithesis of that moment on the footpath when his mouth had first punished her, then aroused her, then stolen her wits.

His mouth descended with tormenting slowness as if he wanted to savour every moment, his lips barely brushing hers, here, there, parting softly in an erotic tango that became darker and deeper as he pulled at her lower lip. He slid his tongue along it, sucked it into his mouth setting up a chain reaction of responses that left her weak, trembling with longing.

Eyes closed, she found his tie, pulled it loose with shaking hands, blindly unfastening studs, scattering them in her desperation to touch his skin, feeling its warmth beneath her hands, against her own.

'Look at me, Claire...'

She opened her eyes and he let his hands slide slowly over her shoulders, brushing aside the straps.

'Look at me...'

His breath was soft against her cheek, his mouth trailed moist kisses down her throat, in the hollow of her shoulder as he slowly lowered the zip.

'Say my name...'

As her dress slithered over her body, pooled around her ankles, Claire let her head fall back in invitation, wanting his mouth on her breasts, wanting it everywhere...

'Dance with me, Hal North,' she murmured, putting her arms around his neck. 'Dance with me.'

CHAPTER THIRTEEN

HAL opened his eyes to the familiar panorama of the Thames, pink in the predawn glow. There were still lights twinkling along the water's edge but scarcely any movement on the river itself.

Beside him, Claire was sleeping, his arm holding her against his chest, his hand cradling a breast. Utterly vulnerable. Completely his. Soon, very soon, she would wake and the perfect moment would be broken in her panic to get home, to be there for Alice, but for now he could watch her sleeping.

'Don't move,' he said as she stirred.

'I don't want to.'

Her body was responding to his own. All he had to do was move his thumb, tease a nipple that was hardening beneath his palm and she'd forget everything, be totally his for another half an hour maybe.

He resisted the temptation, kissed her shoulder. 'I'll make some coffee while you take a shower.'

He rolled away quickly, while he had the strength to let her go, unhooked a gown from behind a door and turned to toss it to her. She had clutched the sheet to her breast, already slipping away from him.

He put the kettle on, bread in the toaster, went to find her something to wear.

'Shirt, sweater, jeans, socks and a new pair of boxers,' he called, dropping them on the bed. 'They'll be a bit on the big side, but they're clean. Shame we didn't bid on that bra...'

His mouth dried as she walked back into the bedroom, bringing with her the scented steam of the shower.

'No problem. It would have been too big for me, anyway.'

'I'm afraid these will be, too, but you'll need them on the bike.'

'Bike?' she said, picking up the pack containing a pair of soft jersey shorts.

'Relax, I don't expect you to cycle home, but by the time a car gets here we can be halfway home.'

'You've got a motorbike?' she asked, a little breathlessly. He hadn't lost her quite yet...

'I'm the local bad boy, remember? Of course I've got a bike.'

She looked up at him. 'You're not bad, Hal...'
'No?'
Her skin was damp, her hair dripping. She smelled of his body wash, his shampoo, she was his and taking a hank of hair, wrapping it round his hand he back her against the wall and proceeded to demonstrate just how bad he could be...

She didn't object as he leaned into her, kissed her, pulled loose the belt of the robe she tied around her so carefully.

Didn't object as he stroked his hand over the length of her body from her neck to the warm, melting apex of her thighs. Holding her with nothing more than his gaze, he stroked her to a juddering climax then wiped his hand across his chest, anointing himself with her essence.

'Not bad...' She had that soft, dreamy smile of a woman completely satisfied. 'Very, very good...'

'Coffee, toast in the kitchen,' he said abruptly before he forgot himself completely. She did that to him. Made him forget who he was, who she was...

Claire roused herself, pulled on the clothes he'd brought her. The too big boxers, a soft woollen shirt that came down practically to her knees. She rolled up the legs of his jeans, cinched in the belt to hold everything together.

There had been a moment, in the middle of the night, when they'd raided the fridge for smoked salmon, champagne, but it took a moment to find the way. Or maybe she wanted the excuse to wander through Hal's lovely apartment, feel the fine Persian rugs beneath her bare feet, touch his things.

A Knole sofa. A Sheraton sofa table with a wonderful bronze of a horse. A Hockney on the wall.

'Had a good look round?' he asked as he handed her a big breakfast cup filled with richly scented coffee.

'You have a beautiful home, Hal. You've come a long way from Primrose Cottage.' Then, when he didn't answer, she said, 'I've never been on the back of a bike.'

'You've never sneaked back into the house at dawn, either. Shame about the leather skirt.'

'You can't have everything.'

'No. There are always sacrifices.' He patted a stool. 'Hop up.' He took the socks she'd been carrying.

'My sandals won't go over them,' she said. 'I thought I might put them over my sandals.'

'No need. I've got an old pair of boots you can have.'

She looked at the pair of biker's boots on the floor beside the central island. 'Those? They're going to be a mile too big.'

'I've stuffed some spare socks in the toes.' He took the socks she was carrying and slipped them on over her feet. Buckled the boots in place. Helped her into a thick, padded jacket, fastening the zip up to the neck.

'I feel like the Michelin man,' she said.

'Do you?' He leaned forward and kissed her. 'Make that a Michelin woman. Come on, it's time to go.'

The drive back to Maybridge was fast, thrilling and Claire clung to Hal like a teenager, her arms wrapped tightly around his middle, leaning into the curves, practically screaming with excitement.

It was madness. She was a mother. She was supposed to be responsible; not flying home at dawn, ripping up the quiet of the village, tearing across the estate, scattering deer, rabbits before Hal finally brought the bike to a swinging, giddy halt by her fence.

He pulled off his helmet.

'Don't move,' he said as she attempted to dismount. For a moment they looked at one another, both remembering when he'd said that before. How his hand had been gently curled around her breast, what she'd wanted…

He slid from the bike, unfastened her helmet, then removed it. Her hair was crushed to her scalp and she pulled off an oversized gauntlet, tried to lift her hand to loosen it. Her arm was stiff, her legs were stiff, too and he lifted her clear of the bike and deposited on the far side of the fence.

'Okay?' he asked, holding her for a moment, then, when he was sure she could support herself, he used one hand to casually vault it, found the spare key, opened the door. And suddenly she didn't know what to say.

'It's a good thing I didn't have to shin up the drainpipe and climb in through the window wearing all this stuff,' she said.

'Easy. You strip off and I take the evidence away with me.' He grinned. 'Want to try it?'

And be caught wearing his underwear by her daughter galloping home at the crack of dawn? 'I'm good, thanks.'

'Sensible answer.'

Yes, well, that was her. Good old sensible Claire.

Except for last night when she'd lost her mind, lost her reason, lost herself.

'Here you go, Cinders,' he said, taking a bag from inside his jacket. Her clothes, her handbag, her shoes.

'Hal…'

He waited.

'See you tomorrow?'

'Tomorrow?'

Today, now, anytime…

'It's the Wish List photo-shoot,' she said. 'Me in the tutu with my magic wand…' She broke off, feeling stupid. 'I thought you might enjoy your big moment.'

'I've had my big moment, Claire,' he said, touching her cheek, briefly. 'Right now I have to get back to London.'

'Oh, but…'

'I've been neglecting things.'

'Of course,' she said. 'Take care.'

She watched him walk away, vault over the fence, fire up the bike, her invitation to stay, have breakfast, left unspoken.

It was just as well. It wouldn't do for her daughter, her neighbour to come walking in on them sharing breakfast.

Sensible Claire would never let that happen.

She swallowed, turned away. Whatever happened now, she would never be the same. Never be that carefully focussed woman who had always only ever had one goal in life.

To pass her exams and be the daughter her mother wanted her to be. To protect her child and be the mother she had always wanted to be. To be good at her job, make a name for herself...

It was like shattering glass.

She'd put herself back together the first time it had broken. When she'd abandoned the strict rules laid down by her mother and her world had fallen apart. Her father had died, her mother had abandoned her.

She'd carefully sealed up the cracks. Learned to focus again. On her baby, her home, her career. Starting at the bottom.

This time was different.

The glass had not just broken, it had fragmented, been blown to the four corners of the wind and in a sudden panic she opened her evening bag, dug out her phone.

There were no missed calls, no messages.

No. She had done the unthinkable and hadn't been struck down by lightning. Yet.

It would be a while before Penny brought Alice home, she could take a nap, catch up on her sleep, but if she went to bed she would think about Hal, dream about Hal.

Instead she changed into jeans that fit, a T-shirt, a pair of Wellington boots, pulled on Hal's woollen shirt over them, rolling up the sleeves. She'd wash it in the morning, but for now she wanted to keep him close.

Look...

Taking her camera, she went for a walk, crossing a footbridge over the Cran, walking along the far bank until she saw exactly why Hal had closed the footpath.

She took photographs using her phone, attached a text to Hal— I looked.

A sort of apology for doubting him.

She told Alice about her evening—some of it—making her laugh about her bidding for a rugby shirt. She gave her the chocolates—hers and Hal's—that she'd saved for her. Then, since there was no response from Hal, she decided to write up a piece for Monday's newspaper about the footpath being undermined by the winter rains.

She thought better of it. She wasn't on the news desk and Hal was right. Nobody actually cared.

'Who are these people?' Alice asked, rooting around in her father's box, picking out one of the photographs.

She glanced at it. 'Some of the men who used to work on the estate when your granddad was alive.'

'And this?'

She glanced at it. It was a picture of a small boy on a pony with a man holding the leading reins. She couldn't think why it was in the box. It was too old to be one of her father's pictures.

'I think the boy is Sir Robert,' she said. 'Doesn't he look sweet?'

'And who is the man?'

His clothes were that of a country gentleman rather than a groom and the posture had a careless arrogance.

'His father, I should think. Sir Harry Cranbrook.'

'Are you sure?' Alice examined it closely. 'He looks an awful lot like Hal.'

Hal?

'It's an old picture, Alice,' she said. 'It can't be Hal.'

'But he has the same hair!'

'Lot's of people have dark hair,' she said, taking it for a closer look. Lots of people had dark hair, but not dark hair that grew in just that way, that slid over the forehead just so. Or a mouth that lifted at the corner...

'And he's the same shape,' Alice insisted.

What?

'Can I keep it?' she asked.

'No.' She took the photograph from her. 'It belongs in granddad's archives.' With his journals. She'd started reading them, but they had just contained weather reports, details of maintenance, hiring and firing of staff, shoot records...

Look...

The phone rang and she snatched it up. Not Hal but Jessie Michaels asking if Alice could go with them to the safari park.

It was all the distraction Alice needed, and forgetting all about the photograph, she rushed off to get changed. She took another look at the photograph.

The same shape?

The same wide shoulders. That way of holding his head. Sir Robert did that, too, but he hadn't had the striking colouring, the strength of features. He'd clearly favoured his mother, although she'd never seen a picture of Sir Harry before.

She'd once asked Sir Robert if there was one

but he'd said it had fallen, been damaged beyond repair.

Looking at this photograph, an entirely different explanation leapt to mind. That the genes had skipped a generation. That the likeness had been too obvious to ignore and he'd removed it.

Was that why Lady Cranbrook had left him? Because he'd had an affair with his cook? She'd always thought of Hal's mother as old, but heading downhill towards thirty herself she had a different view of age.

Looking back it was obvious that she'd been something of a head-turner with her dark, Gypsy looks. Far too much woman for a man like Jack North to handle…

She finally found the entry she was looking for written not in the daily log, but in the back of her father's journal for the year Hal had been banished from the estate.

I did a despicable thing today. I told young Hal North that if he didn't leave the estate Sir Robert would demolish his mother's house. Leave both her and Jack North without a job.

Clearly something had to be done after he rode his bike into the house, parked it in front of the portrait of the man who is, undeniably, his grand-father.

I never liked the boy, he's arrogant, full of himself and helps himself to my game at will, no matter what traps the gamekeepers set, but this was a dreadful thing to do to him. If I had somewhere else to go, I'd leave tomorrow, but the house goes with the job and Sir Robert pays Claire's school fees. Laura would never forgive me for giving all that up on a matter of principle.

One thing I didn't do—destroy Sir Harry's portrait. I've hidden it in the rafters of the hayloft. It's not much, but I've told his mother where it is and, maybe, one day young North will have justice and I will be able to rest easy.

She closed the book, held it close, remembering horrible days when her father hadn't talked to anyone. When her mother had been more demanding. It had passed, but her father had never been quite the same again. She'd always assumed that it was the beginning of the cancer that eventually killed him. But there were other things that ate you up from the inside…

'Mum, where's my…' Alice erupted into the room then came to an abrupt halt. 'Why are you crying?'

She shook her head. 'No reason. I was just re-membering your granddad, Alice. I wish you'd known him. He'd have loved you so much.'

'Sav's got six grandparents,' she said. 'One set got a divorce and married again. She's got loads of aunts and uncles.' She flopped down on a chair. 'Why don't we have any family?'

'Your grandparents were both only children. And grandma... She thought I let her down.' But fam-ily was important and they had so little of it. A few distant cousins. Maybe it was time to build bridges... 'I'll call her later.'

But first she had to call Hal. She wanted him to see this. There were no excuses, but she wanted him to know that her father had loathed himself for what he'd done. That the picture was still there, somewhere.

There was no reply from the house and she hung up when the answering machine cut in; this wasn't something for anyone else to hear.

His mobile phone went straight to voicemail and she left a message asking him to call her back.

Hair done, nails done, make-up done...

Being a fairy wasn't all downside, Claire de-cided. And, in deference to her advanced age, she'd been allowed to choose a ballerina-length dress. Lots of tulle in the skirt and a soft gold bodice with minimal flesh on display. Very family friendly...

Brian was skimming through the photographs on his computer. 'That one, I think.'

'I can live with that.'

He nodded. 'Good, good... We'll need you in full fig at the Mayoral parlour tomorrow morning. His worship wants to gather a little of the glory for himself.'

'Will expenses run to a taxi? I don't fancy travelling on the bus.'

'I'll pick you up if you like.'

'Thanks...' He seemed oddly distracted, seemed unable to look her in the eye. 'Brian, is there something you're not telling me? I do still have a job?'

'What? Oh, yes... You're our star investigative reporter,' he said, attempting a laugh. It wasn't convincing.

'But...' she persisted.

'I shouldn't tell you...'

'What?'

'You'd better see this,' he said, handing her a large envelope. Her heart was beating a little too fast as she put her thumb to the flap, but he stopped her. 'Don't open it here.' Which didn't do her heart rate any favours.

'Actually, I have to get home. I've exchanged babysitting Alice for babysitting puppies.' And this time she was the one attempting the unconvincing laugh.

'Off you go, then. But you didn't get that from me, okay?'

What on earth… She sat on the bench at the bus stop and opened the envelope, peered inside, afraid that it would be covered with red TOP SECRET stickers.

Nothing that exciting.

It was a photocopy of a planning application made by Mr Henry North to demolish the dwelling known as Primrose Cottage, Cranbrook Lane, Cranbrook.

Her house…

The home that she'd made for herself and for Alice.

Hal was going to knock it down. Drive a bulldozer through the rooms that she'd decorated, where she'd hung the curtains she'd made from remnants. The rooms for which she'd bought furniture from junk shops and car boot sales.

He was going to rip up the floors that she'd

sanded, smash the basins whose taps no longer dripped only because she'd taught herself how to change washers, tear out the pipes she'd crawled in the loft, braving spiders to insulate against the cold. Send bulldozers through the garden she had created...

She'd known, when Sir Robert was forced to sell the estate, that her future was uncertain, that her rent would undoubtedly go up. Unlike Sir Robert, Hal was a hard-headed businessman and he was determined that the estate support itself.

She understood that.

But to discover that all the while he was making friends with Alice, making love to her he'd known about this... And not just known about it. This didn't have anything to do with the redevelopment of Cranbrook Park as a hotel and leisure facility. This wasn't the work of some anonymous consultant.

Hal North had planned this. Planned to hurt her as her father had hurt him. Take his pain out on her hide.

I've had my big moment, Claire...

Oh, yes...

It had been a big moment for her, too. She'd thought, hoped that it was more than a one off, but she'd left a voicemail yesterday morning and he hadn't called back.

There had been no texts, no messages.

She'd always known, deep down, that there was something going on, something dark driving him, but she'd forgotten all her misgivings as he'd teased her, romanced her, taken her.

No. Not taken. His ultimate revenge was that she had given herself, heart, body and soul, freely, joyfully.

And now he was gone. Back to London. Back to his real life.

CHAPTER FOURTEEN

CLAIRE'S experience of lagging pipes in the loft stood her in good stead as she searched through the rafters of the elegant eighteenth-century stables—the horses had been housed far more grandly than the humans who did the manual work—for the painting her father had hidden.

Cobwebs, spiders, she brushed them aside without a thought.

It never occurred to Gary to query what she was doing there and when she finally found the crate, nibbled at the corners, covered in dust, cobwebs and mouse droppings, he helped her down with it. Went and found a screwdriver for her so that she could open it.

Being a seventeen-year-old boy, he wasn't interested in a boring old painting of some boring old bloke and went back to the old motorbike he was stripping down.

He looked so young, but Hal was only a few

months older when he'd been turned out to fend for himself.

She turned away. She couldn't afford to think like that, think of him. Only what he was doing to her and Alice, but as she lifted the painting out, peeled back the wrappings, she felt her heart squeeze tight in her chest. Trailed her fingers briefly along the familiar features, the hard cheekbones, that firm jaw...

When had Hal seen it? Discovered the truth? Had his mother told him, or had he found out by chance and ridden into the house, parked his bike beneath it on his eighteenth birthday, an adult staking a claim to his inheritance. Refusing to be ignored...

Scarcely any wonder that Sir Robert had wanted him, this portrait, out of sight.

She stood it up on a bench, took photographs, then carried it inside and left it on Hal's desk.

That done, she went home and, about to become homeless, fired up her computer and had her own 'big moment.'

Henry North Revealed As Son Of Bankrupt Baronet
    It was today revealed that media shy, multimillionaire, Henry North, founder of international

freight company, HALGO, whose background has always been something of a mystery, is the love child of Sir Robert Cranbrook.

As a boy he lived in a humble estate cottage with his mother, Sarah—Sir Robert's cook—and his stepfather, Jack North.

Sir Robert Cranbrook, who refused to acknowledge his son, had him turned off the estate after an infamous incident in which he rode his motorcycle up the steps of the Park and into the front hall on his eighteenth birthday and parking it beneath a portrait of Sir Harry Cranbrook, his grandfather. The portrait, pictured here, and which Sir Robert ordered destroyed, has now been rediscovered hidden in a stable and leaves no doubt of the connection.

In a remarkable turn of fortune, Henry North recently purchased Cranbrook Park—occupied by the Cranbrook family for nearly five hundred years—for an undisclosed sum when creditors forced the sale. Sir Robert, divorced, with no legitimate heir, is now living in a nursing home.

Mr North could not be contacted today for a comment on his plans for Cranbrook Park but he is quoted as saying that, like all his investments, '...it will have to work for its keep...' Local sources suggest that he will use the property as a hotel and conference facility.

This will be just one more step in the history of a property that was granted to Sir Thomas Cranbrook on the dissolution of the monasteries by King Henry XIII for services to the Crown...

It was all there. The potted history of Cranbrook Park, the motorcycle incident, photographs she'd found in her father's box of Hal's mother, his step-father, Sir Robert.

There was the portrait of Sir Harry Cranbrook, beside the head shot of Hal at his desk. There were photographs of Hal at school. A photograph of Primrose Cottage that she'd taken when she first moved in.

All she had to do was call the *Herald,* tell them what she had and she would be paid handsomely for this prime piece of gossip about a man who had, until then, appeared gossip proof.

A fat cheque that she'd need when she was forced to move, a byline in a national newspaper, a chance to move on, be the journalist her mother always wanted her to be.

And if it hurt Hal, well he'd told her himself,

it didn't matter who you hurt as long as you sold newspapers.

She had the phone in her hand. All she had to do was make the call. It was what a real journalist would do.

'Claire? Are you okay? The mayor is waiting for you.'

'I'll be right with you.'

Just press the button. Say the words. What was her problem?

She'd wanted to write his story...

A story about a boy who had made good despite his bad start. A story to inspire. To be proud of.

This was just sleazy gossip. It wasn't the kind of journalist she wanted to be. Looking at this, she realised that right now she would rather be turning her compost heap...

'Look,' he'd told her. Don't just accept what's on the surface. Maybe she'd got it wrong... And if she hadn't she would fight it.

She tossed her phone into her bag and followed the secretary who'd come to hunt her down in the loo.

There was a small group of people in the Mayor's Parlour. Willow Armstrong, who smiled a welcome. The Mayor. The *Observer*'s editor. And Hal North.

'There are you are, Claire,' he said. 'We thought you'd got lost.'

Her mouth moved, but her tongue appeared to be stuck to the roof of her mouth. What on earth was Hal doing here? He was gone, job done...

'Come and stand here. By me.'

On the surface he sounded all charm, his mouth was smiling, but there was no warmth in his eyes and as he rested his hand on her shoulder he leaned close.

'Where were you, Tinkerbell? Counting your pieces of silver?'

'What?'

'Look this way, everyone. Claire, lose the bag, darling and let's see your wand.'

Hal took the bag she was holding and she raised her wand, gave it a little wave.

'It doesn't work,' he said. 'I didn't disappear in a puff of smoke.'

'Okay, big smile... And again... Hold it for one more...'

Hal moved first, his hand around her wrist before she could move. 'If you'll excuse me, Mr Mayor,

I need to have a word with Claire about the project list.'

'Actually, Mr North, I was hoping we might…'

'Call my office,' he said, heading for the door. 'Penny will arrange a time for you to come up to the Hall. Lunch?'

'Oh, yes… Thank you.'

'Hal…'

'Not one word,' he said. 'Not one more word.'

He opened the door of the Range Rover, tossed her bag onto the floor and waited while she climbed aboard, blocking any chance of escape.

He had her wrong. She didn't want to escape. She wanted answers.

If he'd told her he was planning on bulldozing her home into the ground, she wouldn't have fallen in love with him.

How could any woman get it so wrong twice in one lifetime?

When they arrived at the cottage she didn't go around to the back. In the country, the back door was for friends and she stopped at the front, took out her key, as pointed a message as any how angry she was with him. With herself.

Inside, she went straight into the living room—

no more kitchen comfort for him, no more cake—
and turned to face him.

'Why?' she demanded. 'Why are you doing
this?'

'Me?' Apparently she'd taken him by surprise.
She was the one who was supposed to be on the
defensive. 'You're the one who plastered my name,
my family, across the tabloids.'

'Excuse me?'

He tossed a copy of the *Herald* on the table,
open at a headline almost identical to the one on
her computer.

'I didn't write that!'

'You climbed up into the stable loft and found the
picture they've used. Gary helped you. He told me.'

'Hal, I admit that I wrote a story, had it lined up
to send, but it's still in my draft folder. You can see
for yourself.' She didn't wait, but turned and ran
up the stairs, determined to show him. And then,
when she saw the folder was empty, went cold. 'It's
gone.' She turned to him. 'I didn't, I swear. I came
so close, but I couldn't do it. I told you I wasn't a
real journalist…'

She checked the time it had been sent.

'Alice… She was using the computer to surf

stuff for homework. She probably sent an email to Savannah while she was up here…'

'What's this?' Hal said, picking up the planning document.

She glanced at it. 'You should know. It's your application to raze my home to the ground.' She looked up at him. 'What are you going to do, Hal? Sow the ground with salt? Do you really hate my family, me, that much?'

He took the paper, looked at it, and then muttered something scatological.

'Pretty much my first reaction,' she said.

'Where did you get this?'

'Privileged information.'

'Your friend the Chief Planning Officer, I suppose.'

She didn't say a word.

'And the portrait? Where is that?'

'On your desk. Haven't you been home? To the Hall, I mean.'

'I went to straight to the Town Hall. I've been working all weekend with the consultants, making changes to the plans. I wanted to get everything right before I talked to you.'

'Changes?'

'There was your cycle path. The scramble track.

If I can get it through planning.' He looked at the document he was holding. 'Actually, considering this indiscretion I might be able to twist Charlie Peascod's arm.'

'No need. Buy him lunch. He's anybody's for the Red Lion's roast beef.'

'I think that's probably slander.'

'Undoubtedly,' she said. 'Roast beef and a good claret. Are you going to tell on me?'

'I ought to,' he said. He was looking at her, but it was impossible to know what he was thinking. What he would do. 'How did you find out? That Robert Cranbrook was my father.'

'It was Alice who spotted the likeness. I was trying to find something, anything, in my father's journal about you, about what happened, and she picked out an old photograph of Sir Harry. She thought it was you.'

'Did you find anything? In your father's journals?'

'Yes. Dad wrote something the day he made you leave. He was supposed to destroy the portrait but he hid it. He was so ashamed of what he'd done. He told your mother what he'd done. Where it was.'

'She never told me.'

'You'd made your own way. And he didn't deserve a son like you,' she said. 'And now I'm standing in my father's shoes, but shame doesn't undo anything.'

'No…' He took a step towards her.

'I tried to call you, Hal. I wanted to show you, wanted to tell you.'

'I lost my phone on Saturday night. Apparently I dropped it in the hotel. Leaving in a hurry…' He dragged his hand over his face. 'This morning is not going the way I planned.'

'No. Me, either. I didn't expect to see you. I thought you'd just been stringing us all along. That Saturday night was part of it…'

'I can see why you might think that. A few weeks ago you might have been right.' He drew in a slow breath. 'You would have been right. I was going to evict you, smash this place down, clean the earth…'

'It was that bad?'

'Yes, Claire, it was that bad. Jack North knew he was a cuckold and he made my mother pay every day he lived. Drank every penny she earned. All she kept from him was the money Cranbrook gave her to get rid of me.'

'But she didn't. And she saved the money for when you needed it.' She reached out a hand to him. 'That's what you meant, isn't it? When you said it was extraordinary?'

He took her hand, drew her close so that they were leaning against one another, supporting each other.

'Why did she stay, Hal?'

'Passion?' he suggested. 'I used to roam the house as a boy and I saw them once...' He drew in a long, shuddering breath. 'He said that she was a whore. When he signed the contract on this place. Called me trash—'

'No, no!'

'I could have forced the paternity issue at any time, but I never wanted that man as my father. I just wanted him to look at me, see me, to know in his heart—always assuming he had one—that he'd made a mistake...'

'What changed, Hal?'

'I told myself that I wouldn't have to look you in the eyes when I evicted you. You didn't matter enough for that.' He eased back so that he was looking straight at her. 'But then Archie got into the act and I was looking into your beautiful grey eyes and I was so angry with you, because you did matter.'

'Did I?'

'Then you took out a ten-pound note to bribe me and that was fine, because I could be angry with you all over again.'

'It was all I had to last me until the end of the week, but it wasn't that. I was so disappointed in you. I was so sure that you were bigger than that...'

'And then I saw what you'd done here and hell, I was still angry because I needed to destroy this place.'

'And now?' she asked. 'Do you still feel that way?'

He lifted his hand to her cheek, laid her head against his chest. 'It's not the house, Claire. It's not Cranbrook Park. He said it would destroy me, said that my anger would eat me up, leave me hollow... Maybe it would have, but for you.'

'And now everyone knows and it's all my fault...'

'Who cares? Tomorrow some footballer will cheat on his wife and all this will be nothing more than something to wrap the potato peelings.'

She looked up. 'It's going to be "no comment," then?'

'Always. But there is one thing,' he said, wrapping both his arms around her, holding her close.

'Oh?'

'I'm afraid you're going to have to sacrifice some of your garden.'

Her garden. She was going to be staying...

'Actually, I'm doing you a favour,' he assured her.

'Oh. How, exactly?'

'You're going to be busy organising the restoration of the Rose Garden at Cranbrook Park to be double digging your vegetable plot.'

She would? 'I will?'

'Double digging is so last century,' she said. 'What plans do you have for my garden?'

'I'm going to extend Primrose Cottage.'

'Extend it?'

'Think about it, Claire. Four dogs, two adults, a little girl who's growing every day. Then there's your office, my office. It's just not going to be big enough.'

Four dogs, two adults...

'The Hall isn't big enough for you?'

'I'm not going to live in a hotel.'

'So you've decided you'll move in with me?'

'It's a start. Of course it will be very tight until the extension is finished. People will talk...'

'The sofa is a pull-out...'

'I want a home, a family, Claire. I've found what

I've been looking for and it's you.' His blue eyes burned with a fire that heated her to her toes, stole her breath, made her feel as if her wings were real… 'The deal is marriage. Not a practise run until something better comes along, not a tryout, but the real till-death-us-do-part deal. That's the one wish that only you can grant.'

'I'm a novice fairy, Hal. I haven't been issued with my fairy dust…'

'Forget fairy dust, a kiss will work all the magic we need,' he said. And he waited.

She lifted her arms and wrapped them around his neck.

'Marriage, forever…'

'Marriage, forever…'

And he was right. They had no need of fairy dust, because as her lips touched his, and her dream came true, the world turned gold.

They were married in the ruins of the ancient abbey in Cranbrook Park on the last weekend in August.

Alice and Savannah were bridesmaids, Penny was matron of honour. The bride's mother and the groom's mother outdid one another in the hat department.

There was no pink.

According to the reporter from the *Observer,* the only member of the press invited to the wedding—well, apart from the entire staff—the bride was wearing a dress of silver grey lace with a sash of a blue that exactly matched the groom's eyes.

The bridesmaids were wearing dresses in the same material as the sash. The dogs, a donkey and a pony had bows, ditto.

The groom must have been wearing something but the only thing anyone noticed was his smile.

* * * * *

Mills & Boon® Large Print

September 2012

A VOW OF OBLIGATION
Lynne Graham

DEFYING DRAKON
Carole Mortimer

PLAYING THE GREEK'S GAME
Sharon Kendrick

ONE NIGHT IN PARADISE
Maisey Yates

VALTIERI'S BRIDE
Caroline Anderson

THE NANNY WHO KISSED HER BOSS
Barbara McMahon

FALLING FOR MR MYSTERIOUS
Barbara Hannay

THE LAST WOMAN HE'D EVER DATE
Liz Fielding

HIS MAJESTY'S MISTAKE
Jane Porter

DUTY AND THE BEAST
Trish Morey

THE DARKEST OF SECRETS
Kate Hewitt

Mills & Boon® Large Print

October 2012

A SECRET DISGRACE
Penny Jordan

THE DARK SIDE OF DESIRE
Julia James

THE FORBIDDEN FERRARA
Sarah Morgan

THE TRUTH BEHIND HIS TOUCH
Cathy Williams

PLAIN JANE IN THE SPOTLIGHT
Lucy Gordon

BATTLE FOR THE SOLDIER'S HEART
Cara Colter

THE NAVY SEAL'S BRIDE
Soraya Lane

MY GREEK ISLAND FLING
Nina Harrington

ENEMIES AT THE ALTAR
Melanie Milburne

IN THE ITALIAN'S SIGHTS
Helen Brooks

IN DEFIANCE OF DUTY
Caitlin Crews

912 Rom LP